NUTCRACKER

E.T.A. Hoffmann
NUTCRACKER

Illustrated by Patricia Seminara

ISBN 0-86622-325-8

Book Design: Patricia Seminara

Published by Paganiniana Publications, Inc.
211 West Sylvania Ave.
Neptune City, New Jersey 07753

Contents

CHAPTER I

Christmas Eve

All through the afternoon of Christmas Eve Dr. Stahlbaum's children had not been allowed into the dining-room, much less into the drawing-room opening out of it. In a corner of the back-parlour Fred and Mary sat cuddled up together, shuddering with the excitement of mystery, for, though twilight had come on, nobody, this evening, brought in any lights. Fred whisperingly told his sister how, since early in the morning, he had listened to the stir and the bustle and the soft hammerings in these forbidden chambers, also how, not long ago, a small, dark man, with a great box under his arm, had come slipping over the floor. But he knew well that this couldn't be anyone other than Godfather Drosselmeier. Then Mary clapped her hands for joy, crying:

'Ah! what fine things will Godfather Drosselmeier have made for us?'

Counsellor Drosselmeier, so people called him, was far from a handsome man, short and thin, with many wrinkles on his face, and a great black patch where his left eye should have been. Also, he had no hair on his head, so he wore a very fine white wig, which seemed to be all made of glass, so clever a piece of work was it.

The godfather himself, indeed, was a very clever work-man, who actually knew all about clocks and could even make them with his own hands. When any of the fine clocks in the Stahlbaums' house went out of order and did not strike, Godfather Drosselmeier would come, take off his glass wig and his drab coat, tie on a blue apron, and stick sharp things into the clock's in-sides, so that little Mary felt quite sorry for it. This did the clock no harm, which, on the contrary, had come alive again and at once began to tick, strike, and chime, to the delight of all the family. He never came without bringing something pretty in his pockets for the chil-dren—now a puppet that could move its eyes and make bows, most comic to behold; now a box out of which would hop a little bird, or something else of the kind. But for Christmas he always prepared some grand elab-orate piece of work that cost him much trouble, on which account, when given to the children, it was care-fully taken charge of by their parents.

'Ah! what fine things will Godfather Drosselmeier have made for us?' Mary wondered, but Fred thought that this time it had to be a castle, in which all kinds of beautiful soldiers marched up and down, and were drilled. Other soldiers were to come, who should try to get into the castle, but then the soldiers inside would fire off cannon, and there would be such a grand boom-ing and banging.

'No, no!' Mary cut him short. 'Godfather Drossel-meier has told me of a beautiful garden with a great pond in it, on which splendid swans with gold bands round their necks are to swim about and sing such pret-ty songs. Then a fair, young maiden will run up from the garden, and call the swans to her and feed them with gingerbread.'

'Swans don't eat gingerbread!' broke in Fred, rather rudely, 'and Godfather Drosselmeier could not make a whole garden either. Anyhow, we get few of the toys he makes, they are always taken away from us. I like much better the things papa and mamma give us, which we have for our very own, and can do as we like with them.'

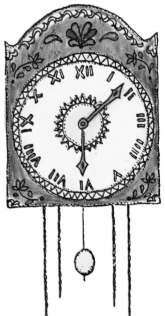

Then the children went on guessing and guessing what it would be this time. Mary remarked how Missy Gertrude, her big doll, was much changed for the worse, since she kept tumbling on the floor more awkwardly than ever. This never happened without leaving dirty marks on her face, and as for keeping her clothes clean, that was out of the question. All the scoldings in the world thrown away on her! Fred, for his part, dwelt on the fact that a fine wooden horse was much wanted in his stable, also how his toy soldiers were greatly deficient in cavalry, as his father must be aware.

These children knew well that their parents had bought for them all sorts of fine presents, yet they were persuaded that Father Christmas looked on them with friendly eyes, and bestowed, with great generosity, the gifts that came more welcome now than at any other time. As they kept on whispering over the expected presents, their eldest sister Louisa came to remind them that it is Father Christmas who, through the hands of their dear parents, always supplies what will afford them real joy and pleasure, as he knows better how to do than children themselves. Louisa continued that they should therefore not be wishing and hoping for all sorts of things, but should quietly and happily await what is to be given them. Mary became thoughtfully silent, but Fred murmured to himself:

'I should like a horse and some hussars, though!'

It had grown quite dark. Fred and Mary, sitting closely side by side, did not dare to speak a word. They fancied they could hear a fluttering of soft wings about them, and a strain of beautiful music in the distance. A bright light gleamed upon the wall. Then they knew that Father Christmas was flying away on shining clouds to other happy children.

All at once a silvery bell went *kling, kling*, the doors flew open, and such a brilliance streamed out of the great room that the children stood as if enchanted on the threshold, with loud exclamations of wonder. But papa and mamma came forward and took Fred and Mary by the hand, saying:

'Come along, come along, dear children, and see what Father Christmas has given you!'

CHAPTER II

The Presents

I put it to you, my friendly reader or listener, and beg you to bring clearly before your eyes your own last Christmas tree or table adorned with pretty, gay presents. Then you can very well understand how these children stopped, dumfounded, with sparkling eyes. How only after a little, Mary cried with a deep sigh of delight: 'Oh, how beautiful! Oh, how beautiful!' and how Fred jumped for joy being unable to contain himself. All the past year, indeed, they must have been particularly good and well-behaved, for never had they had such a number of delightful presents as this time.

The great Christmas tree in the middle bore ever so many gold and silver apples, and for buds and blossoms, every branch hung thick with almonds and brightly-colored sugar-plums and other best kinds of goodies. But the finest thing about the marvellous tree must not be forgotten, that a hundred small lights twinkled like stars among its foliage, so that, illuminated as it was inside and outside, it seemed to invite the children to pluck its fruits and flowers. And round about the tree everything shone gay and splendid; all the fine presents there—who could ever describe them? Mary caught sight of the most elegant dolls, all sorts of neat little dolls' furniture, and, what seemed finest of all, a silk frock prettily decked with colored ribbons stood spread out on a dress-stand before her eyes, so that she could admire it from every side, as she did, crying out again and again, 'Oh, how pretty! Oh, what a beautiful dress! And can I—may I really put it on?'

Meanwhile Fred, galloping and trotting round three or four times, tried his new wooden horse, which he indeed found bridled and saddled on the table. Dismounting, he reported that it was a wild creature, but no matter, he would soon break it in, and proceeded to muster his new squadron of cavalry, who were gorgeously equipped in red and gold, with silver swords, and rode such shiny white horses that these also might almost be believed of pure silver.

The children had overcome their excitement a little, and were able to take a look at the picture-books which lay open so as to display pretty flowers and brightly-colored figures of people, even of dear little children at play, painted as naturally as if they really lived and spoke. Yes, Fred and Mary were settling down upon these wonderful picture-books, when the bell rang again. They knew that now it was Godfather Drosselmeier's turn, and ran to the table standing by the wall.

The screen that had so long concealed it was quickly drawn away, and what did the young folks see? On a green lawn, bespangled with gay flowers, stood a most noble castle, all plate-glass windows and gilded towers. A chime of bells was heard, doors and windows flew open, and you saw how very tiny but most elegant ladies and gentlemen, with feathers in their hats and trailing skirts, moved inside the rooms. In the central hall, that seemed to be on fire, so many lights burned there in silver chandeliers, children wearing short coats and vests were dancing to the music of the chimes. A gentleman in an emerald-green cloak kept looking out through a window, nodding and disappearing by turns, while a figure, just like Godfather Drosselmeier himself, but scarcely higher than papa's thumb, would, from time to time, come and stand at the castle door and then go in again.

With his arms leaning on the table, Fred had examined the dancing and walking figures, and now he said:

'Godfather Drosselmeier, will you let me go into your castle?'

The Counsellor replied to him that this would never do. Indeed, he spoke truly, for it was foolish of Fred to want to go into a castle which, gilded towers and all, was not so high as himself. Fred had to admit that. After a time, as the ladies and gentlemen went on walking up and down in the same way, the children dancing, the green man looking out at the window, Godfather Drosselmeier's likeness coming to the door, he cried impatiently:

'Godfather Drosselmeier, now will you come out for once at the other door?'

'That won't do, dear Fred,' answered the Counsellor.

'Well,' said Fred again, 'just make the green man, who looks out so often, walk about with the others.'

'That won't do either,' repeated the Counsellor.

'Couldn't the children come downstairs?' persisted Fred. 'I should like to see them nearer.'

'Oh, all that won't do!' said the Counsellor, not in very good humor. 'The machinery has to work as it is made.'

'Is that the way of it!' exclaimed Fred in a tone of contempt. 'Nothing will do! I tell you what, Godfather Drosselmeier, if your fine little figures in the castle can only go on doing the same things, they are not worth much, and I don't particularly care about them. No! I would rather have my hussars. They can maneuver forwards, backwards, as I like, and are not shut up in a house.'

And with this he ran to the table, and made his squadron on their silver horses trot up and down, and wheel and charge and shoot to his heart's content.

Mary also had quietly slipped away, for she, too, soon grew tired of the strutting and capering of the puppets in the castle, but was so polite and good-natured that she would not show it so plainly as her brother Fred. Counsellor Drosselmeier spoke rather crossly to the parents.

'Such a skillful contrivance is not for senseless children. I will pack up my castle again.'

But the mother came forward, and got him to show her the construction and the wonderfully ingenious works by which the little puppets were set in motion. The Counsellor took it all to pieces and put it together again. This put him into a rather better temper, and he presented the children, furthermore, with some pretty brown men and women made of gingerbread, with gilt faces, hands, and legs, which quite delighted them.

Louisa had, by her mother's wish, put on the handsome dress which was her present, and looked very nice in it. But when Mary was to try on her new frock, she thought she would rather look at it a little longer, and they allowed her to have her own way.

CHAPTER III

A Peculiar Pet

Mary, in fact, could not tear herself away from the table of presents, since she had just discovered on it something, till now unseen. The marching off of Fred's hussars, previously paraded close in front of the Christmas tree, left exposed to view a very remarkable little man, who stood still in the background, as if quietly awaiting his turn for notice. His figure, indeed, was not much to be proud of, for his rather long thick body by no means fitted his small thin legs and his head also seemed far too big. His nice clothes, however, which bespoke a person of taste and cultivation, went far to make up for this deformity. He wore a very fine, shiny, violet hussar jacket, with many white buttons and braidings, trousers of the same stuff, and the most elegant boots that ever adorned the feet of a dandy student or, for that matter, of an officer. They fitted his neat little legs as closely as if painted on them. Very peculiar it was indeed that he also wore behind him a short, stiff cloak which looked exactly like wood, and a funny cap on his head. It reminded Mary of Godfather Drosselmeier who also wore on occasion an unappealing lounging-jacket and a dreadful cap, yet was a dear, good godfather for all that. It also occurred to Mary that being dressed similarly, something about the nutcracker made him appear more handsome to her than godfather.

As Mary kept looking harder and harder at this mannequin, who had quite taken her heart at first sight, she came to perceive a kind nature and an inner warmth expressed on his face. His clear, blue, and certainly too prominent eyes bespoke nothing but friendliness and benevolence. It suited his looks well that his chin bore a well-trimmed beard of white cotton, which set off the pleasant smile on his bright-red mouth.

'Ah, papa!' cried Mary at length, 'who is to have this dearest little man on the Christmas tree?'

'That,' said her father, 'that fellow, my dear child, is to make himself useful to you all. His work is to crack hard nuts for you, and he belongs to Louisa as much as to Fred and to you.'

With this her father carefully took the figure off the table, and, lifting up its wooden cloak, made the little man's mouth gape open to show two rows of very sharp white teeth. Then he told Mary to put in a nut, and with a twist and a sharp *crack* it had been broken so that the shell fell in pieces, and Mary got the small kernel in her hand. Now Mary understood that the elegant little man was one of a long line of Nutcrackers, and practised the profession of his ancestors. The little girl cried out for joy, when her father said:

'Since this fine fellow pleases you so much, dear Mary, you shall be in charge of his care and protection, though, as I said, Louisa and Fred have as much right to use him as you.'

Mary at once took him into her arms, and made him crack nuts. Yet Mary always picked out the smallest ones, in order that her new found friend might not have to stretch his mouth so wide open, which she did not think good for him. Louisa came to look, and for her also Friend Nutcracker had to perform his service, which he seemed to do with goodwill, for he appeared to be smiling in a most warm and friendly way.

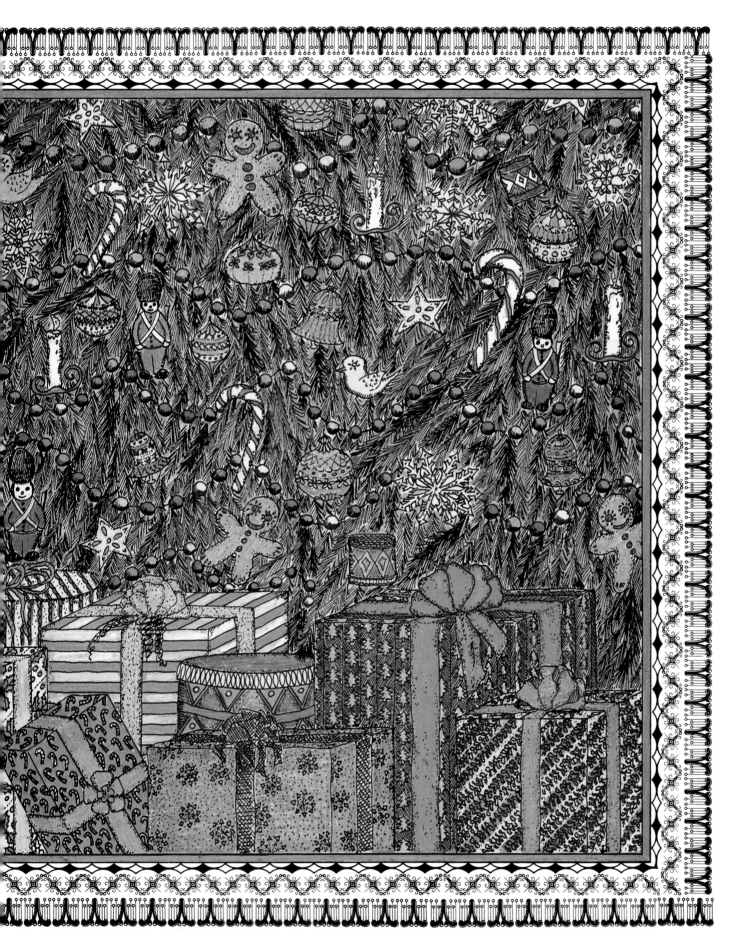

Meanwhile, Fred had grown tired of all his riding and drilling, so, when he heard such a pleasant cracking of nuts, he ran to his sisters and laughed heartily at the funny little man, who was passed from hand to hand, and was never allowed to stop opening and shutting his mouth.

Fred always kept shoving in the biggest and hardest nuts, but, all of a sudden there was a splintering noise and three teeth fell out of Nutcracker's mouth, as well as rendering his lower-jaw loose and wobbly.

'Oh, my poor dear Nutcracker!' cried Mary, snatching him out of Fred's hands.

'What a silly, stupid fellow!' exclaimed Fred. 'Sets up for being a nutcracker, and hasn't a good set of grinders! He doesn't seem to be very first-rate at his business. Hand him over, Mary! I'll make him go on cracking nuts for me, even if he loses all his teeth and his whole chin into the bargain, which is all that good-for-nothing deserves.'

'No, no!' cried Mary in tears. 'I won't let you have him. Just see how sadly he looks at me. He looks like he is in pain. You are so cruel! You beat your horse, have your soldiers shot, and now you want to torture my Nutcracker.'

'That's real life. You don't understand these things,'

answered Fred. 'Besides the Nutcracker belongs to me as much as to you. Hand him over here!'

Mary began to cry bitterly, and hurried to wrap up the wounded Nutcracker in her small pocket-handkerchief. Her parents and Godfather Drosselmeier interfered. The latter, to Mary's grief, took Fred's part, but her father said:

'I have put Nutcracker under Mary's protection, and since, as I see, he now needs it, she has full power over him, and nobody is to say a word against her. Besides, I am very much surprised at Fred that he should require fresh duty of a man injured on service. As a good soldier, he ought to know that wounded men are never put in the ranks.'

Fred was much ashamed of himself, and, without troubling further about nuts or Nutcracker, slipped off to the other side of the table, where his hussars had been camped for the night, after posting the proper guards.

Mary picked up Nutcracker's lost teeth. Round his hurt chin she bound a nice white ribbon, taken off her dress, and then wrapped the poor little fellow, who looked very pale and dejected, more carefully than ever in her pocket-handkerchief. Thus she held him, nursing him like a baby in her arms, while she turned over the pretty picture-books which lay among the rest of the presents. She became quite angry, as was not at all usual with her, when Godfather Drosselmeier laughed a great deal, and kept asking how she could go on so with that hideous little creature. The strange resemblance to Drosselmeier which had struck her at first setting eyes on her Nutcracker, came again into her mind, and she spoke quite seriously:

'Who knows, Godfather, whether you, if you were to make yourself as fine as this poor fellow, and had as nice a jacket on, who knows whether you would look as handsome as he does!'

Mary did not understand why her parents laughed so loud, or why the Counsellor got so red in the face and did not join in the laugh as heartily as before. There may have been some particular reason for this.

CHAPTER IV

Marvels

n the parlor at Dr. Stahlbaum's, on the left-hand side as you go in at the door, stood a high glass cupboard, where the children kept all those fine things that were given them every Christmas. Louisa was quite a little girl when their father had the cupboard made by a very clever carpenter, who put in so many panes of clear glass that the treasures inside looked almost brighter and prettier than when you had them in your hands. On the highest shelf, out of Fred and Mary's reach, stood Godfather Drosselmeier's works of art; right beneath was the shelf for the picture-books; the lowest compartments Mary and Fred could fill with what they pleased. Mary had taken the bottom shelf as the dwelling of her dolls, and Fred's troops used the one over it as their barracks.

Such was now the arrangement. While Fred quartered his hussars above, Mary laid Missy Gertrude by in a corner below, and set out the new, finely-dressed doll in that well-furnished apartment, and invited herself to take goodies with her.

Very well furnished was the apartment, I have said, and it is true, for I know not if you, my attentive reader, possess such a fine flower-print sofa, several fashionable little chairs, a small tea-table, and above all a very neat clean little bed, for your dolls to take their rest in. All this was in one corner of the cupboard shelf, whose walls here were even papered with pretty pictures. You can easily believe that the new doll, who, as Mary learned the same evening, was named Miss Clara, found herself very comfortable in this apartment.

It was late in the evening, getting on for midnight indeed, and Godfather Drosselmeier had long gone home, and yet the children could not tear themselves away from the glass cabinet, for all their mother's telling them it was time to go to bed.

'To tell the truth,' cried Fred at length, 'my hussars would like some rest now, and so long as I am looking at them I know that not one of them dare nod!'

With this he went off, but Mary earnestly begged:

'Only a little while, dear mother, let me stay here only a little longer; I have so much still to look after. As soon as I have finished I will go straight to bed.'

Mary was a very dutiful, sensible daughter, so her good mother could leave her alone among the toys without being fearful. But in case of her being so much enchanted by the new doll and the other playthings, as to forget the candles burning by the cupboard, her mother put them all out. Only the lamp, which hung from the ceiling in the center of the room, spread a soft, pleasant light around.

'Come soon to bed, dear Mary, or you will not be up in good time in the morning!' called out the mother, as she went off to her own bedroom.

When Mary found herself alone, she quickly set about what she had in mind to do. She didn't know why, but she did not care to be seen by her mother. All this time she had been nursing the injured Nutcracker in her arms, wrapped in a handkerchief. Now she laid him carefully upon the table, softly, softly unwrapped him and examined his injuries. Nutcracker was very pale, but yet he smiled with such an air of melancholy kindness that it went right to Mary's heart.

'Ah, dear little Nutcracker!' she murmured, 'don't be angry with my brother Fred for hurting you so much; he did not mean any great harm. He is only rather un-feeling through that rough soldier-life, but in other ways a real kind-hearted boy, I can assure you. But now I will take very good care of you till you have grown quite well and happy again. Your teeth shall be put in firm, and your shoulder set straight by Godfather Drosselmeier, who understands these things—'

So Mary was going to say, but could not finish the sentence, for, as she mentioned the name of Drossel-meier, Friend Nutcracker made an ugly, cross face, and his eyes seemed to shoot out green sparkles. Then, just as Mary was ready to feel terrified out of her wits, there again she saw the worthy Nutcracker's face as placid as ever with its melancholy smile, and now she knew that a draught in the room, making the lamp flicker, must have so altered his countenance for a moment.

'I must be a very silly girl to be so easily frightened. I actually believed this wooden figure was making faces at me! But I am really getting so fond of Nutcracker, he is such a funny and such a good-natured fellow; and so he must be properly nursed as he deserves.'

With this she took Nutcracker on her arm, ap-proached the glass cupboard, bent down before it, and thus addressed the new doll:

'I beg you very particularly, Missy Clara, to give up your bed to the sick, wounded Nutcracker, and manage as well as you can on the sofa. Remember that you are quite well and strong, or you would not have such plump, red cheeks, and that very few of the hand-somest dolls possess so soft sofas as you have.'

Missy Clara, in all her Christmas finery, looked very stuck-up and sulky, and did not answer a word.

'Why should I make so much work about it?' ex-claimed Mary, drawing forward the bed, where she laid Nutcracker very gently and softly, bound up his in-jured shoulder with a pretty little ribbon from her own dress, and covered him snugly with the bed-clothes up to his nose.

'He is not to stay beside that selfish Clara,' she said, and lifted bed, Nutcracker, and all on to the shelf above, so that he lay close to the pretty village of toy houses in which Fred's hussars were quartered.

She closed the cupboard, and was going off to her bedroom, when there began a soft, soft whispering and stirring and rustling all round her, behind the stove, behind the chairs, behind the cupboard. The clock ticked louder and louder, and gave a whir as if it were going to strike, but did not. Mary looked at it—the great gilded owl which sat on the top had let down its wings so as to cover the whole clock face, at the same time stretching out its ugly cat-like face and its hooked beak. And more loudly came the ticks as plain as words:

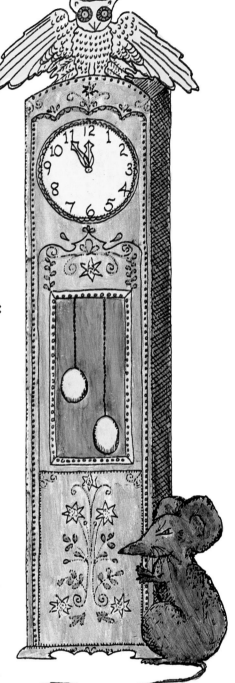

    'Clock, clock, click!—Low, softly tick!
Mouse-king's ears are quick!
Pirr, pirr—ting, tong!
Sing out the old song!
But strike in a low tune!
It will be over soon!'

And the clock chimed twelve times, but dully and hoarsely, as if its notes were muffled.

Mary began to creep all over, and in her fright she was on the point of running away, when she saw how Godfather Drosselmeier seemed to have taken the place of the owl, his drab coat hanging down on both sides like wings. Yet she made an effort to be brave, and called out, almost crying:

'Godfather Drosselmeier, Godfather Drosselmeier, whatever are you doing up there? Please come down because you're frightening me.'

But now there broke out from all sides a wild creaking and squeaking, and soon, behind the walls, there came the sounds of a thousand tiny marching feet, accompanied by a thousand little lights shining through the cracks in the floor. They were not candles—no!—but small sparkling eyes; and Mary perceived that a host of mice were everywhere peeping forth and working themselves out. Presently they were going trot, trot, hop, hop, round the room. Troops of mice, always

growing more numerous and spirited, galloped up and down, and at length formed themselves in ranks, as Fred was accustomed to draw up his troops, when he gave orders for a battle. This struck Mary as very comical as she was not afraid of mice, like many other children. However, all at once there came a squeak so piercing and startling that an ice-cold shudder ran down her back.

Oh! What did she now see? Yes, indeed, my worthy reader, I know that your heart is as much in the right place as that of the clever and brave field-marshal Fred Stahlbaum but, all the same, had you only seen what came before Mary's eyes, you would have run away on the spot. I believe you would even have jumped quickly into bed and drawn the clothes farther over your ears than there was any need for.

Ah! that is just what Mary could not do, for—would you believe it?—right under her feet burst up sand and lime and crumbled stone, as if thrown out by some subterranean power, and from the floor arose seven mouse-heads with seven glittering crowns, hissing and squeaking terribly. Before long the body also squeezed itself clear and the huge seven-crowned mouse shrieked with all his throats, three times piping out a greeting to his army, that at once set itself in motion, and charged straight upon the cupboard, straight upon Mary, who still stood by its glass front.

The girl's heart had been beating so violently for distress and terror that she believed it would soon burst and she would die. But now all the blood seemed to freeze in her veins. Half-fainting she staggered back— something went *crash*—and the pane of the cupboard, which she had struck with her elbow, was shattered to pieces. At the same moment she felt a smarting pain in her right arm, but at once a weight seemed to be taken off her heart, for she heard no more squeaking and shrieking. All had become still, and, though she feared to look, she thought the mice, scared by the crash of glass, must have scurried back into their holes.

But what happened next? Right behind Mary there

arose a strange stir and bustle in the cupboard, and tiny voices began to be heard:

'Awake, awake!
Arms to take!
This is the night!
Rouse for the fight!'

And then pealed out a pleasant, pretty chime of bells.

'That is my little bell-toy!' cried Mary joyfully, springing quickly up to look.

Now she saw how the cupboard was lighted up in some wonderful fashion, and how all its inhabitants were on foot. There were several figures there, besides the dolls, running about in confusion and striking with their little arms. All of a sudden, Nutcracker jumped up, threw the blankets far away, and sprang to his feet on the bed, shouting loudly his war-cry of defiance:

Knick, knack, knack!
Stupid mousey-pack!
Krick, krack, whack!
Haw, hick, and hack!

And with this he drew his little sword and waved it in the air, and cried:

'You, my dear soldiers, friends, and brothers, will you stand by me in the hard battle?'

At once spiritedly replied three clowns, a pantaloon, four chimney-sweepers, two fiddlers, and a drummer:

'Yes, lord, we hold to you with steadfast loyalty,— with you march we to death, victory, and combat!'

And they pressed after the courageous Nutcracker, who ventured a dangerous spring from the upper shelf.

They, for their part, could well manage the jump, for not only were they thickly clothed in cloth and silk, but there was nothing inside of them but cotton and bran, so down they plumped as softly as feather pillows. But the poor Nutcracker, he would surely have broken arms and legs, for, remember, it was nearly two feet high from the shelf on which he stood to the one below, and his body was as brittle as a toothpick. Nutcracker would surely have broken his limbs, had not, at the moment he leaped down, Clara sprung from

the sofa, and in her soft arms received the hero with his drawn sword.

'Ah, dear, kind Clara, how have I mistaken you!' sobbed out Mary. 'I am sure you must have given up your bed to the fearless Nutcracker with a good will, after all.'

And now Missy Clara said, pressing the young hero gently to her silken breast:

'Oh, sir, will you, sick and wounded as you are, yet expose yourself to combat and peril? See how eager for the fray are your bold men, and how they troop themselves as certain of victory. Clowns, pantaloon, chimney-sweepers, fiddlers, and drummer are already down below on the field and the soldiers in my compartment are all astir, preparing for the fight. Will you not, dear sir, rest in my arms, or behold the battle from this lofty perch?'

Thus spoke Clara, but Nutcracker could not be restrained, kicking so hard that the doll had soon to let him go and set him on the ground. Immediately then he knelt gallantly on one knee, murmuring out:

'Fair lady, ever in the thick of the combat will I remember the grace and favor you have shown me!'

At this Clara bent down low, seized him by both arms, lifted him softly up, and loosened her richly-spangled sash which she intended to place over his shoulder. However, he took two steps backwards, laying his hand upon his chest and spoke with formal politeness:

'Do not deign, oh lady, to waste your favors on me—' Here he stopped short, sighed deeply, tore from his shoulder the ribbon with which Mary had bandaged him, pressed it to his lips, hung it round him as his crest and then, bravely brandishing his glittering unsheathed sword, sprang, light and active as a bird, over the ledge of the cupboard on to the floor.

You remark, kind and honored reader, that Nutcracker, even before he really became alive, must have deeply felt the affectionate goodness with which Mary had treated him. And on this account only, because Mary was so kind, he would not take or wear a token from Missy Clara, splendid and beautiful as it was. The true-hearted Nutcracker chose rather to adorn himself  with Mary's simple ribbon.

But what now is going to happen? As soon as Nutcracker sprang down, the squeaking and pattering broke out again. Ah, under the big table swarm the deadly squadrons of countless mice and over all towers the frightful seven-headed Mouse King! How will the battle go?

CHAPTER V

The Battle

'Sound the general march, my trusty drummer!' cried Nutcracker at the top of his voice. At once the drummer began to pound the drum that caused the panes of the cupboard to shake and echo. Now came a crashing and clattering within, and Mary perceived that the lids of the various boxes in which Fred's army had been quartered were thrown off, and out sprang the infantry down on to the lower shelf, where they fell into shining ranks. Nutcracker flew up and down, urging on the troops with spirit.

'No dog of a trumpeter to be found!' he exclaimed angrily but straightway turned to the Pantaloon, who had grown somewhat pale, with a tell-tale chattering of his long chin, and addressed him in solemn tones: 'General, I know your courage and your experience. Here quickness of eye and decision are all-important. To you I entrust the command-in-chief of the cavalry and the artillery. You don't need a horse, as you have such long legs, and can gallop along on them well enough. Now attend to your duty!'

Forthwith Pantaloon pressed his long dry fingers upon his mouth, and gave such a piercing crow that it rang like the notes of a hundred shrill bugles. There arose in the cupboard a neighing and trampling as though a herd of wild horses were about to be unleashed. Suddenly, Fred's cavalrymen and dragoons, but, before all, the new gaily-equipped hussars, emerged, soon coming to a halt on the floor below.

Now, with flying flags and clanging music, regiment after regiment defiled before Nutcracker, and drew themselves up in three lines obliquely across the room. Then Fred's cannon were advanced rattling, to the front, with their gunners about each and presently they began to explode with their fire power and Mary saw how their sugar-plum shot plunged into the masses of the mouse army, who became powdered all over and put greatly to shame. But particularly they suffered severe loss from a battery of heavy guns which had taken up its position on mamma's footstool, and with relentless profusion kept volleying out gingerbread nuts among the mice, causing many casualties among the mice hordes.

The mice, however, steadily advanced and even overran the forward lines of Nutcracker, taking a few of the guns. Still there resounded the deafening sound of the cannon—till for smoke and dust Mary could scarcely see what was going on. Yet this much was certain, that each army fought with the utmost determination, and that victory wavered from one side to the other.

The mice kept on drawing out fresh forces, while their fire, very well delivered, took effect even as far as the glass cupboard. Clara and Gertrude ran up and down in despair, and wrung their hands till they were sore.

'Am I to die in my blooming youth, I, the fairest of dolls?' screamed Clara.

'Have I for this so carefully preserved my looks, to perish here within the walls of my home?' cried Gertrude.

Then they fell clinging to one another and lamenting so loudly as to be heard over all the wild tumult of the battle. For, worthy reader, you can scarcely have any idea of the scene that now raged. Cannon and musket fire continued to pour forth from both sides in a tor-

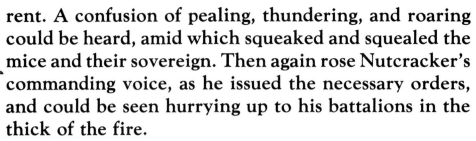

rent. A confusion of pealing, thundering, and roaring could be heard, amid which squeaked and squealed the mice and their sovereign. Then again rose Nutcracker's commanding voice, as he issued the necessary orders, and could be seen hurrying up to his battalions in the thick of the fire.

General Pantaloon had made some most dashing cavalry charges, and gloriously distinguished himself. But Fred's hussars were driven back by the mouse-artillery, which left deadly marks on their red jackets, and this checked their ardor. Pantaloon drew them off by the left, and in his excitement he himself, with his cavalry and dragoons, executed the same movement, that is to say, they all retreated and went home. Thus the battery posted on the footstool became endangered, and before long a heavy column of fierce ugly mice charged it so resolutely that footstool, guns, and gunners were all lost. Nutcracker seemed confounded by dismay, and ordered the right wing to make a retrograde movement.

During the hottest of the fight, masses of mouse-cavalry had been quietly emerging from under the chest of drawers, and with loud horrid squeaks had furiously hurled themselves upon Nutcracker's left wing. There they met with stiff resistance. Slowly, owing to the nature of the ground, it being difficult to pass the cupboard ledge, had the regiment of infantry advanced under the leadership of two Chinese Emperors, and formed themselves in square. These spirited, gaily-equipped, and noble troops, consisting of many Gardeners, Highlanders, Japanese, Barbers, Harlequins, Cupids, Lions, Tigers, Baboons, and Apes, fought coolly, courageously, and steadily. By their Spartan bravery would this choice regiment have wrested the victory from the foe, had not a daring captain of the hostile cavalry, rushing recklessly forward, bitten off the head of one of the Chinese Emperors. The latter, in his fall, knocked over two Japanese and a Baboon. This made a gap through which the enemy broke into the square, and soon the whole regiment was bitten to pieces. Yet the conquerors gained little advantage by this butchery. As soon as any of their bloodthirsty troopers had bitten a bold adversary in two, he swallowed tiny pieces of paper which choked the mice causing their abrupt demise.

This did not much avail Nutcracker's army, which, retreat once begun, became more and more completely routed, and lost men faster and faster, till the unfortunate Nutcracker, with a very small band of his comrades, was brought to bay close in front of the glass cupboard.

'Bring up the reserves! Pantaloon, clown, drummer, where are you?' So shouted Nutcracker, who yet hoped to see fresh troops pouring out of the cupboard.

There did come out, indeed, a few brown men and women, made of gingerbread, with gilded faces, hats, and helmets. But they were so clumsy that they struck none of the enemy, but instead knocked off the cap of their commander Nutcracker himself. The light troops opposed to them soon bit through their legs, so that they tumbled down bringing some of their own comrades with them.

Closely surrounded by foes, Nutcracker was now in the utmost danger and distress. He would have sprung back into the cupboard, but his legs were too short. Clara and Gertrude lay in a swoon and could not help him. Hussars and dragoons galloped over him, as he cried in despair:

'A horse! A horse! My kingdom for a horse!'

At that moment two of the enemy's skirmishers seized him by his wooden cloak, and up rushed the Mouse King, squeaking out triumph from all his seven throats.

'Oh, my poor Nutcracker!' sobbed out Mary, unable longer to restrain herself. Hardly knowing what she did, she snatched off her left shoe and violently flung it at the Mouse King, right into the middle of his troops. That moment, all appeared to grow dim and to vanish away. But Mary felt in her right arm a still sharper pain than before, and fell fainting on the floor.

CHAPTER VI

Laid Up

hen Mary awoke out of her deep death-like sleep, she was lying in her own bed, and the sun appeared shining clear and bright into the room through the windows covered with frost. By her side sat a strange gentleman, whom, however, she presently recognized as a surgeon.

'She is awake now,' said he softly, and up came her mother, regarding her with anxious looks of inquiry.

'Oh dear mother!' murmured little Mary, 'are all the mice gone, then, and is good Nutcracker safe?'

'Don't talk such silly stuff, Mary,' answered her mother. 'What have the mice to do with a Nutcracker! But, you naughty child, you have given us all a great deal of trouble and anxiety. That comes of children having their own way and not obeying their parents. Last night you were playing with your toys very late. You grew sleepy, and it may be you were frightened by a mouse jumping out—though there used to be no mice here. Anyhow, you struck your arm against the glass of the cupboard and cut yourself so badly that this gentleman, who has just taken out the bits of glass sticking in your arm, says your injury might have been fatal if the glass had cut a vein. Thank God that I woke in the middle of the night. I found that you were not in bed, got up and went into the parlour. There you lay senseless beside the cupboard, and were bleeding fast. I had almost fainted away myself for fright, to see you lying among a number of Fred's lead soldiers, toys, and gingerbread men. But the Nutcracker lay on your cut arm, and your left shoe was not far off.'

'Ah, dear mother, mother!' broke in Mary, 'these were the remains of the great fight between toys and mice, and what alarmed me so much was the mice trying to take Nutcracker prisoner, who commanded the toy-army. Then I threw my shoe among the mice, and after that, I know no more of what happened.'

The surgeon looked meaningfully at her mother, who said very gently to Mary, 'Never mind, my dear child! Keep yourself easy; the mice are all gone, and Nutcracker is safe and sound in the cupboard.'

Here Doctor Stahlbaum came into the room, and had a long conversation with the surgeon. Then he felt Mary's pulse, and she could make out that they were talking about fever.

She had to lie in bed and take medicine, and this lasted for several days, although, except for the pain in her arm, she did not feel much the matter with her. She knew that Nutcracker had come out of the battle safely, and he often appeared to her as in a dream, speaking quite plainly but in a very sad voice:

'Mary, dearest lady, I am deeply indebted to you, but there is yet more which you can do for me.'

Mary thought a great deal over this speech, but had no idea what it might be that she could do for him.

She was not able to play much with toys, on account of her wounded arm, and if she tried to read or to turn over picture-books, there came such a strange swimming in her eyes that she had to leave off. So time passed wearisomely slow for her, and she had scarcely patience to wait for the twilight hour which came so welcome, for then her mother sat on the bed a while and read or told her such pretty stories.

One evening her mother had just finished the most entertaining history of Prince Charming, when the door opened, and in came Godfather Drosselmeier with these words:

'Now I must really see for myself how my sick and wounded Mary is getting on.'

As soon as Mary saw Godfather Drosselmeier in his drab coat, there returned to her a clear memory of that night when Nutcracker lost the battle against the mice. She could not keep herself from crying out aloud to the Counsellor:

'Oh, Godfather Drosselmeier, you were so ugly! I saw you very well, sitting over the clock and covering it with your wings to prevent it from striking loudly, not to scare away the mice. I heard you very well calling to the Mouse King! Why didn't you help Nutcracker and me? How could you let the mice succeed? Isn't it all your fault, then, that I have to lie sick and wounded in bed?'

'Whatever is the matter with you, dear Mary?' asked her mother, quite startled.

But Godfather Drosselmeier made some very queer faces, and snarled out a sort of sing-song, thus:

'Pendulum, tick, tick,
Clock, clock, click, click,
Hammer goes dong, ding,
Hour rings out ting, ting,
Hunt away Mouse King!
Owl spreads her light wing,
Toys now may dance and sing,
Clock strikes out ting, ding,
All the works click, click,
Pendulum goes tick, tick,
Click, tick, whir, pir-r-r,
Bim, boom, bang, bir-r-r,
Ding, dong, so ends my song!'

Mary stared at Godfather Drosselmeier with eyes opened to their widest, for he looked quite different, and even much uglier than his usual self, and moved his right arm up and down as if he were pulling the strings

of a puppet. He would have really terrified her if her mother had not been there, and if presently Fred, having slipped in meanwhile, had not burst out into a loud laugh.

'Oh, Godfather Drosselmeier, you are so funny to-day!' he cried. 'You are going on exactly like my old Jumping-Jack, which I threw away behind the stove a long time ago.'

But their mother said, looking serious:

'Dear Mr. Counsellor, this is a strange kind of fun! What may be the meaning of it?'

'Dear me!' answered Drosselmeier, laughing; 'don't you remember my pretty Clockmaker's song? I am in the way of singing it always to patients like Mary.' Then he sat down close to Mary's bed, and said: 'You must not be offended if I have not cut out all the Mouse King's fourteen eyes, but that is out of the question, and instead of it I am going to give you something that will bring you great pleasure.'

With this the Counsellor put his hand into his pocket, and what he now ever so slowly drew forth was none other than the Nutcracker, whose lost teeth he had very cleverly set in firm again, and mended his broken jaw! Mary cried out for joy, and her mother said with a smile:

'You see now how well Godfather Drosselmeier meant by your Nutcracker.'

'That you must admit, Mary,' interrupted the Counsellor, 'and you must concede also that Nutcracker has not grown quite so straight as he might have done, and that his looks can't be called handsome. If you care to hear it, I will tell you how this ugliness came into his family. Or perhaps you already know the history of Princess Pirlipat, of the mouse-queen, and of the skillful Clockmaker?'

'Just listen,' suddenly broke in Fred, 'just listen, Godfather Drosselmeier. You have put in Nutcracker's teeth right enough, and his chin is no more so wobbly, but why is his sword gone—why have you not given him a sword?'

'Eh!' replied the Counsellor, not very well pleased. 'You fuss and find fault about everything, youngster. What business of mine is Nutcracker's sword? I have healed his body, and he can get a sword for himself as he pleases.'

'That's true,' cried Fred. 'If he is a brave fellow, he will soon manage to find weapons.'

'Well, Mary,' went on the Counsellor, 'tell me if you know the story of Princess Pirlipat.'

'Ah, no!' answered Mary. 'Do tell us it, dear Godfather Drosselmeier, do tell us.'

'I hope,' said the Doctor's wife, 'I hope, dear Mr. Counsellor, that your story is not such a *creepy* one as those you tell usually.'

'Not at all, dearest lady,' answered Drosselmeier. 'On the contrary, what I am going to have the honor to relate to you is very amusing.'

'Do tell us, oh do, dear godfather!' cried the children, and the Counsellor thus began his tale.

CHAPTER VII

The Story of the Hard Nut

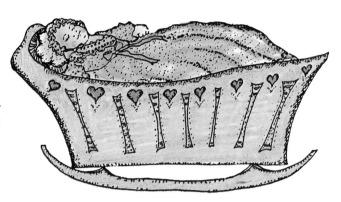

irlipat's mother was the wife of a King—that is, a Queen; and Pirlipat herself was a born Princess from the moment of her arrival. The King went wild with joy over his lovely little daughter as she lay in the cradle. In his exultation he danced and whirled about on one leg, and cried out over and over again:

' "Hurrah! Has anybody ever seen anything more beautiful than my Pirlipatkin?"

'Then all the Ministers, Generals, Presidents of Departments, and Staff-Officers hopped about on one leg, like their sovereign, crying with all their might:

' "No, never!"

'But indeed it was not to be denied that in all the world there could be no more beautiful child than Princess Pirlipat. Her little face seemed to be woven out of delicate lily-white and rose-red silk, her eyes were brightly-sparkling blue, and it was pretty to see how her hair curled like shining threads of gold. Besides, had Pirlipatkin brought into the world two small rows of pearly teeth, with which, an hour or two after her birth, she bit the High Chancellor's finger as he bent down to examine her features closely, so that

he shrieked out loudly, "Oh, Gemini!" Others maintained that he cried out "Oh dear!" and opinions are strongly divided on the point to this day. But the fact is, Pirlipatkin actually bit the High Chancellor's finger, and the enraptured nation now recognized that wit, spirit, and intelligence all at once dwelt in her little angelic body.

'In short, everybody was delighted. Only the Queen showed herself anxious and ill at ease but nobody knew why. It seemed strange that she had Pirlipat's cradle watched so carefully. Not only were the doors guarded by men-at-arms, but, without counting the two nurses beside the cradle, six others had to sit round about in the room night after night. Then, what appeared quite ridiculous, and what no one could understand, each of these six nurses must sit with a cat on her lap, and stroke it so as to keep it purring all night.

'You could never guess, dear children, why Pirlipat's mother took all these precautions, but I know, and I will tell you now.

'It happened that once a number of illustrious kings and highly-distinguished princes had assembled at the court of Pirlipat's father, on whose account there were grand doings, including many tournaments, plays, and court dances. The King, in order to prove beyond doubt that he had no lack of gold and silver, was advised, for once, to dip deeply into the crown treasures and bring out something worthy of the occasion. To this end, being privately informed by the Chief Cook that the Court Astronomer had announced a propitious day for pork-butchering, he ordered a great making of meat puddings and sausages, then jumped into a carriage that he might personally invite the collected kings and princes—only to a plate of soup! as he put it, the better to enjoy their surprise over the costly banquet. Next he addressed the Lady Queen in his most winning tones:

' "It is well known to you, my dear, how fond I am of sausage meat."

'The Queen knew very well what he was hinting at. It was that she, as she had often done before, should undertake the serious cookery business with her own royal hands. The High Treasurer must at once send the great golden sausage-pot and the silver stew-pans to the kitchen. A huge fire of sandal-wood was kindled there. The Queen tied on her damask cooking apron and soon all the pots and pans steamed with the sweet odors of pudding-making.

'Right up to the Council Chamber stole this tempting smell, till the King, seized by hearty delight, could not restrain himself.

' "Excuse me, my lords!" he exclaimed, flew quickly down to the kitchen, kissed the Queen, did a little stirring in the pot with his gold sceptre, and then went back well pleased to the Council.

'Now the important moment had arrived when the bacon should be cut into little bits and broiled upon a silver gridiron. The court ladies stood aside, since the Queen, out of loyalty and respect for her royal husband, would endeavor to perform this task alone. But as soon as the bacon began to sputter, a tiny wee whispering voice made itself heard:

' "Give me, too, some of your bacon, my sister—I'm a queen like yourself. Give me some of the bacon!"

'The Queen knew well that it was Lady Mouseykins who spoke thus. Lady Mouseykins had lived for many years in the king's palace. She declared herself related to the royal family, and that she was queen in the realm of Mousedom, wherefore she also kept a great court under the hearthstone. Now our Queen was a kind good-natured lady, and while she would not exactly recognize Lady Mouseykins as a queen and her sister, she had not the heart to begrudge her a taste of the nice things on feast days, and called out:

' "Come along, Lady Mouseykins; you may always taste the bacon."

'Out popped Lady Mouseykins very smartly, jumped on to the hearth, and with her pretty little paws snapped up one shred of bacon after another which the Queen held out to her. But next came leaping forth all the uncles and cousins of Lady Mouseykins, and into

the bargain her seven sons, right mischievous scamps, who threw themselves on the bacon, not to be kept off for all the frightened Queen could do. Luckily the Chief Lady-in-Waiting arrived to the rescue, and hunted away these troublesome guests, so that some of the bacon was still saved from their clutches, which had to be scientifically divided among the sausages after the directions of the Court Mathematician, called in for the purpose.

'Trumpets and kettle-drums resounded, as the invited potentates and princes came in gorgeous robes of state to the sausage feast, some on white ambling palfreys, and some in crystal coaches. The King welcomed them with hearty friendliness and courtesy, then took his place, bearing the royal crown and sceptre, at the head of the table.

'When the white puddings were first served, it could be seen that his Majesty was disappointed. Violent pangs were evidently raging within him.

'But when they reached the course of black puddings, he sank back in his arm-chair, sobbing and moaning. He covered his face with his hands and broke forth into loud lamentations.

'All present sprang to their feet. The court Physician in vain made an effort to feel the King's pulse. He seemed convulsed by some deep, nameless anguish. Finally, after many suggestions, after the use of strong remedies, burning of feathers under his nose, and such like, his Majesty, being so far brought to himself, stammered out almost inaudibly these words:

' "Too little bacon!"

' "Oh, my poor, unhappy royal husband!" sobbed the disconsolate Queen, throwing herself at his feet. "Ah, what pain must you be suffering! But here you see the guilty one before you, punish her severely! Ah! Lady Mouseykins it was, with her seven sons, her uncles and cousins, who have eaten up the bacon, and —" thereupon the poor Queen fell back in a swoon.

' "Chief Lady-in-Waiting, how was this?" cried the King, rising up full of wrath.

'The Chief Lady-in-Waiting related what had happened as well as she could, and the King vowed to take revenge on Lady Mouseykins and her family, who had eaten up the bacon out of his sausages.

'The Privy Council being summoned, it was resolved to prosecute Lady Mouseykins and to confiscate her property. But as the King considered she might meanwhile go on eating his bacon, the matter was at once placed in the hands of the Court Clockmaker.

'This man, who was named, exactly like myself, Christian Elias Drosselmeier, undertook, by means of a singular piece of state-craft, to banish Lady Mouseykins and her family forever from the royal palace. He contrived, accordingly, certain small artfully-constructed machines, in which shreds of toasted bacon were fastened upon a thread, and these Drosselmeier placed round about the habitation of the bacon-nibblers.

'Lady Mouseykins was much too clever not to see through his cunning, but all her warnings, all her lectures were thrown away on her seven sons, and many, many of her uncles and cousins, who, enticed by the sweet smell of the bait, ventured within Drosselmeier's machines. Then, as soon as they tried to gnaw away the bacon, the mice found themselves trapped by a grating that fell suddenly behind them. They were summarily delivered to shameful execution in the very kitchen where they had enjoyed such pleasant feasts.

'With her small band of surviving subjects, Lady Mouseykins abandoned the scene of horror. Woe, despair, and revenge filled her breast. The courtiers exulted, but the Queen was troubled, knowing the nature of Mouseykins, and too well aware that she would not leave her sons and kinsmen unavenged.

'Indeed, as her Majesty was one day cooking a fricassee of chicken, a dish much loved by her kingly husband, Lady Mouseykins appeared and said:

' "My sons, my cousins, and kinsmen are dead; take good heed that the Mouse Queen bite not thy little Princess in two—take good heed! Ha! ha!"

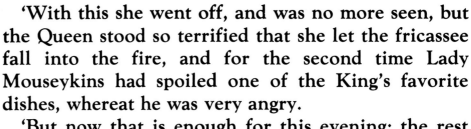

'With this she went off, and was no more seen, but the Queen stood so terrified that she let the fricassee fall into the fire, and for the second time Lady Mouseykins had spoiled one of the King's favorite dishes, whereat he was very angry.

'But now that is enough for this evening: the rest another time.'

Earnestly as Mary, who had her own ideas about this story, begged Godfather Drosselmeier to go on with it, he would not let himself be persuaded, but jumped up, saying:

'Too much at once is not good: more tomorrow.'

Then, as he was just going out of the door, Fred asked:

'But do tell us, Godfather Drosselmeier, is it really true that you invented mouse-traps?'

'How can you talk such nonsense?' cried his mother; but the Counsellor laughed in his queer way:

'Am I not a clever clockmaker; and must not mouse-traps have been invented somehow or other?'

CHAPTER VIII

The Story of the Hard Nut (continued)

 ow you see, children,' so the Counsellor continued next evening, 'why the Queen had the wonderfully beautiful little Princess Pirlipat watched over with such care. Was she not right to fear that Lady Mouseykins would fulfil her threat by coming back to bite the royal baby in two? Drosselmeier's machines were of no use at all against the cautious and crafty Mouse Queen and only the Court Astronomer, who was also Privy Interpreter of Omens and Stars, could divine that the family of Puss and Purr had the power of keeping off mice from the cradle. So it came about that a great number of these cats were employed by the Court and were each held on her lap by each nurse, whose duty was to tickle him into contented performance of such laborious public service.

'It was the midnight hour, as one of the Nurses-in-Chief, who sat close to the cradle, started up from a deep sleep. All around lay buried in slumber—there was no murmur. It was as silent as death itself. You can therefore imagine the feelings of the Chief Nurse when, right before her, she observed a great ugly mouse standing on its hind paws, and laying its murder-

ous head on the face of the Princess! With a cry of horror she sprang to her feet. Everyone awoke, but in an instant Lady Mouseykins—the huge mouse on Pirlipat's cradle could be no other—scampered off to a corner of the room. The four-footed Chamber Councillors rushed after her, but too late! She had vanished through a crack in the floor. Then at the noise Pirlipat awoke, weeping piteously.

' "Thank heaven!" cried the nurses. "She is still alive!"

'How great was their dismay, however, when they looked at Pirlipat, and saw what had come to the sweet tender child! Instead of the angelic white and red curly-haired pate, a thick, distorted head stood on a small, shrunken, crooked body. The sky-blue eyes had changed into green goggling balls staring straight before them and the pretty little mouth gaped from ear to ear.

'The Queen was ready to die for weeping and lamentation, and the King's study had to be hung with wadded tapestry, since again and again he ran his head against the wall, exclaiming in most lamentable tones, "Oh, unlucky monarch!"

'You would likely expect that the King would believe it were better to eat his sausages without bacon, and to leave Lady Mouseykins and her kindred in peace beneath the hearthstone. But Pirlipat's royal father had no such thought, rather he threw all the blame on the Court Clockmaker and Engineer, Christian Elias Drosselmeier of Nuremberg. Therefore he sagely gave command as follows: Within four weeks must Drosselmeier restore the Princess to her former state, or at least suggest some trustworthy means of doing so, else should he suffer a shameful death under the executioner's axe.

'Drosselmeier was in a panic, yet soon he took courage to trust his art and his good luck, and at once set about the first operation which seemed to him likely to be of use. He very skilfully took Pirlipat to pieces, screwed off her hands and arms, and examined her construction inside. From this he was disappointed to discover that the bigger the Princess grew the more unshapely she would become, and he could hit on no way of mending the matter. He carefully put the Princess together again, and sank in gloomy dejection upon her cradle, which he dared not to leave day or night.

'The fourth week had come, it was already Wednesday, when the King found the unfortunate engineer and, with angry eyes, and, shaking his sceptre at him, cried:

' "Christian Elias Drosselmeier, set the Princess to rights, or you will die!"

'Drosselmeier began to weep bitterly, but the little Princess Pirlipat went on contentedly cracking nuts. For the first time the Clockmaker was struck by Pirlipat's unusual appetite for nuts, and by the circumstance that she had come with teeth into the world. Indeed, after her transformation, she had gone on screaming just till she happened to have a nut given her, which she at once cracked, ate the kernel, and then became quiet. Since then the nurses could never bring enough nuts for her.

' "Oh, sacred instinct of nature, eternal mysterious sympathy of all existence!" exclaimed Christian Elias Drosselmeier. "Thou showest me the gate of the secret; I will knock, and it will open!"

'He forthwith sought permission to consult the Court Astronomer, and was taken to him under a strong guard. The two officers embraced each other with many tears, being devoted friends, then retired into his private laboratory to examine many books which dealt with dark mysteries as instinct, sympathy and antipathy.

'Night coming on, the Royal Astronomer consulted the stars, and, with the help of Drosselmeier, also well versed in the same art, drew out Princess Pirlipat's horoscope. This proved a hard task, for the lines of fate became more and more entangled as they went on. But at last, it became clear that to destroy the enchantment which had so hideously deformed her, and to be made

as beautiful as ever, the Princess Pirlipat had nothing to do but to eat the sweet kernel of the nut Crackatuck!

'The nut Crackatuck had such a hard shell that a forty-eight pound cannon could be driven over it without breaking it. This hard nut must be cracked by the teeth of a man who had never shaved and never worn boots, and he must hand it to the Princess with his eyes shut, and not open them till he had taken seven steps backward without stumbling.

'Three days and three nights did Drosselmeier and the Astronomer work unceasingly, and it was only on Saturday, at the King's dinner-time, that Drosselmeier, who was to be beheaded on Sunday, burst in, full of triumphant joy, to announce the discovery of the means for restoring the Princess's lost beauty. The King, embracing him with warm affection, promised him a sword set in diamonds, four Orders of Chivalry, and two new Sunday coats.

' "Immediately after dinner set about the business," he bade. "See to it, dear Engineer, that the young unshaved man in shoes is provided with the nut Crackatuck and let him drink no wine beforehand, for fear of his stumbling when he takes seven steps backward like a crab. After that he can soak himself to his heart's content."

'Drosselmeier, upon listening to the King's speech again became frightened and, not without consternation and trembling, he stammered forth that the means of cure indeed were discovered, but that the nut and the young man to bite it were still to be found. Indeed, there was some doubt whether nut and nutcracker would ever be found.

' "Then you must be beheaded after all!" roared the King in a lionvoice, wrathfully brandishing the scepter above his crowned head.

'Lucky it was for poor Drosselmeier that the King had enjoyed his dinner that day, so as to be in good humor for listening to the arguments which the magnanimous Queen did not fail to bring forward in favor of one whose sad fate had touched her heart. Drosselmeier plucked up courage, and represented on his own part that he had duly fulfilled the task set him, and had earned his pardon by pointing out how the Princess could be cured. The King said this was all nonsense but finally decided, after he had taken a glass of stomach-cordial, that both the Clockmaker and the Astronomer should set forth, not to return without the nut Crackatuck in their pockets. The man to bite it open, as the Queen suggested, must be sought for through repeated insertions of an advertisement in the home and foreign newspapers.'

Here the Counsellor again broke off, promising to relate the rest next evening.

CHAPTER IX

The Story of the Hard Nut (concluded)

ext evening, as soon as the candles were lighted, Godfather Drosselmeier made his appearance, and went on with his story as follows:

'Fifteen years were Drosselmeier and the Court Astronomer on their travels, without discovering even a trace of the nut Crackatuck. Where they wandered far and wide, what strange wonderful things they fell in with, all this I could go on telling you for a month, but will do nothing of the kind. Enough to say that the soretroubled Drosselmeier was at length seized by a mighty longing for his native place, Nuremberg. This longing one day overpowered him, as he sat in a great wood in Asia, smoking a pipe of canaster with his friend.

' "Oh, my beautiful mother city,
Who never has seen thee is much to pity!
Though he travel to London, to Rome, to
   Berne,
After thee his heart must always yearn—
After thee, O Nuremberg, town so dear!
That hath beautiful houses and windows
   clear!"

'As Drosselmeier lifted up his voice so dolefully, the Astronomer was moved to deep sympathy, and began to give forth such lamentable howls that they could be heard over a great part of Asia. Then, composing himself, he wiped the tears from his eyes, and asked:

' "But, my worthy colleague, why do we sit here and cry? Why not go to Nuremberg, since no one forbade us to search for the fated Crackatuck there?

' "That's true enough," answered Drosselmeier.

'Both at once stood up, knocked the ashes out of their pipes, and went off in a straight line, without stopping, from the wood in the middle of Asia to the city of Nuremberg.

'Scarcely had they arrived there than Drosselmeier hastened to his cousin, the dollmaker, varnisher, and gilder, Christopher Zacharias Drosselmeier, whom he had not seen for many, many years.

'To him now the Clockmaker related the whole history of Princess Pirlipat, of the Lady Mouseykins, and of the nut Crackatuck, so that he struck his hands together, and cried out, full of astonishment:

' "Ah, cousin, cousin, what a wonderful story!"

'Drosselmeier went on to tell of the adventures of his long travel, how he spent two years with the Date King, how he was contemptuously turned away by the Prince of Almonds, how he made inquiries in vain of the Natural History Society in Squirrels' Town, in short how everywhere he had failed to get even a hint about the nut Crackatuck.

'During this narration, Christopher Zacharias had kept snapping his fingers, turning about on one foot, clicking with his tongue, then exclaiming—"H-m! H-m!—Ah!—Eh!—Oh!—The deuce!" Finally he threw his cap and wig up into the air, warmly embraced his kinsman, and cried out:

' "Cousin, cousin, you are saved—saved you are, I say for unless I am much mistaken, I myself possess the nut Crackatuck."

'At the same time he pulled out a box from which he drew forth a gilded nut of middling bigness.

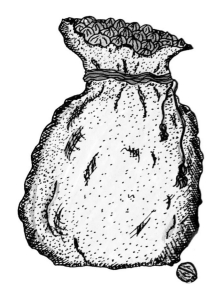

' "See!" he said, showing the nut to his cousin. "This is the state of the case. Years ago a foreigner came to me at Christmas-time, with a sackful of nuts which he wanted to sell. Right before my shop, he got into a quarrel, and laid down the sack that he might better defend himself against the nutsellers of the town, who would not allow a stranger to sell nuts here, and attacked him on this account. At that moment a heavily-loaded wagon rolled over the sack, and all the nuts were broken except one, which the foreigner, with a queer smile, offered me in exchange for a small silver coin of the year 1720. It struck me as odd that I found in my pocket just such a coin as the man wanted, so I bought the nut and gilded it, hardly knowing myself why I paid so dear for the thing and treated it as of such value."

'All doubt of the cousin's nut being that long-sought-for one became at once removed, when the Astronomer, summoned into council, cleverly scraped away the gilding, and on the rind of the nut found engraved in Chinese characters the word Crackatuck. Great was the joy of the travellers, and the cousin the happiest man under the sun, when Drosselmeier assured him of his fortune being made for, besides a good pension, he should henceforth receive gratis all the gold leaf he needed for his gilding.

'Both the Clockmaker and the Astronomer had already put on their night-caps and were going to bed, when the latter, that is the Astronomer, thus began:

' "My beloved colleague, one piece of luck comes not alone. Believe me, we have found not only the nut Crackatuck, but also the young man who can crack it and restore the Princess to her beauty! The man is none other than the son of your worthy cousin. No, I will not sleep," he continued enthusiastically, "but this very night will cast the youth's horoscope." Therewith he tore off his night-cap, and at once set about taking observations.

'The cousin's son was indeed a nice, well-grown young man, who had never yet shaved or worn boots. In his earlier youth, he had acted as an acrobat for several Christmases, but that was not in the least perceptible, as his father had gone to great lengths to educate him and set him straight. At Christmas-time he wore a fine red coat laced with gold, a sword, a hat under his arm, ? .d a first-class head of hair gathered into a "pony-tail". So splendidly adorned, he stood in his father's shop, and out of natural politeness cracked nuts for the young ladies, on which account they called him the handsome little nutcracker.

' "It is he!" cried the Astronomer the next morning, joyously cavorting about the room. "We have him! We found him! But two things, dearest colleague, must be seen to. In the first place, you must provide your excellent nephew with a strong wooden head having an under jaw that will stand a good strain. Then, on arriving at the capital, we ought to keep it carefully secret that we have brought along with us the young man to bite open the nut Crackatuck. He should come on the scene some time later. I read in the horoscope, that the King, after some others have broken their teeth over it to no purpose, will promise the hand of the Princess and succession to the kingdom, as reward for whoever can crack this nut and restore Pirlipat's lost beauty."

'Drosselmeier's cousin the dollmaker was well content that his youngster should marry the Princess Pirlipat and become a prince and a king, and he left the whole charge of the business to the messengers. The head, which Drosselmeier fitted on to his hopeful young nephew, turned out very well, so that he made most successful experiments at cracking the hardest peach stones.

'As soon as Drosselmeier and the Astronomer announced at the palace their arrival with the nut Crackatuck, the necessary advertisements were at once published. Travellers from far and wide consisting of many fine young men, some of them princes, eagerly came forward, trusting in their sound jaws to undertake Pirlipat's disenchantment.

'The messengers were not a little horrified when they saw the Princess again. Her small body, with its shrunken members, could scarcely support the huge unshapely head, while the hideousness of her features was enhanced by a white woolly beard that had grown over her mouth and chin.

'All happened just as the Court Astronomer had read in the horoscope. One youngster in shoes after another bit away at the nut Crackatuck till he broke his teeth and jaws, without doing the Princess the least good, and as each was then borne away, half-fainting, by the dentist kept ready at hand, he would moan out:

' "That *was* a hard nut!"

'When finally the King, despairing to cure his daughter, promised her hand and his kingdom to whoever would perform the disenchantment, there presented himself that pretty lad from Nuremberg, and modestly begged permission to make a trial. None of the candidates had pleased the Princess so much as young Drosselmeier. She laid her little hand on her heart and sighed deeply:

' "Ah, if only it were he who should bite open the nut Crackatuck and become my husband!"

'After most civilly saluting the King and Queen, and also the Princess Pirlipat, young Drosselmeier took the nut Crackatuck from the Chief Master of Ceremonies, put it between his teeth, worked his head powerfully, and *crack-crack*! the shell broke into several bits. Dexterously picking from the kernel the rough fibres about it, he handed it to the Princess with a respectful scrape of his foot, then closed his eyes and began to step backward. The Princess at once swallowed the nut and instantaneously the deformity was gone, and there in its place stood an angelic figure, the face dimpled rosy-red and lily-white, the eyes of shining blue, the long locks curled like threads of gold!

'Music of trumpets and kettle-drums swelled the loud exultation of the people. The King and his whole court danced on one leg as at Pirlipat's birth, and the Queen had to be treated with smelling salts having fainted away in her joyous raptures.

'Young Drosselmeier, who had still the seven steps

backwards to accomplish, was not a little alarmed by this great tumult, yet he kept his balance, and stood raising his right foot for the last step, when Lady Mouseykins, squeaking and squealing shrilly, ran out of the floor, so that in the act of setting down his foot, he trampled upon her, which made him stumble, and he had almost fallen.

Suddenly the youth had become as deformed an object as Princess Pirlipat before. His body had shrunk up, and could scarcely bear the weight of the big un-shapely head with great eyes staring out of it, and broad, horribly-gaping mouth. Instead of his fine bunch of hair, hung behind him a kind of narrow wooden cloak with which his lower jaw was worked.

'Clockmaker and Astronomer were stricken with dread and amazement, yet they saw how Lady Mouseykins rolled all bleeding on the floor. Her ill nature had not gone unpunished, for, with the sharp heel of his shoe, young Drosselmeier had trodden so hard on her neck that she must die. And, writhing in her death-agony, she squeaked and squawked pitiably:

' "Oh, Crackatuck, hard nut that proves my end! Ah, Nutcracker, thy hour is now at hand! Hee! Hee! Woe's me! But also woe to thee! My son, the Mouse King with the seven crowns, will soon avenge his murdered mother's wrongs on thee, thou ugly, spoiled, conceited doll! Oh, life so fair and bright, from which I fall to shades of gloomy death—I fail for breath! My last I speak!—Oh! Ah! Eh! *Squeak!*"

'With this cry expired Lady Mouseykins was carried out by the royal fire-tender.

'At first no one had noticed what had happened to young Drosselmeier, but now Pirlipat reminded the King of his promise, and at once he ordered the hero of the day to be brought forward. But when the unfortunate fellow showed himself in all his deformity, the Princess held both hands before her eyes, crying:

' "Away, away with the hideous Nutcracker!"

'Forthwith the High Marshal seized him by his narrow shoulders and threw him out at the door. The

King, full of rage that a Nutcracker should be forced upon him as son-in-law, put all the blame on the Clock-maker and the Astronomer, and banished them for ever from his capital.

'That had not appeared in the horoscope which the Astronomer cast at Nuremberg, but he did not fail to make fresh observations, and now read in the stars that young Drosselmeier might take heart in his new condi-tion, for, in spite of his deformity, he should yet become a prince and a king. His unshapeliness, how-ever, could disappear only when the seven-headed heir of Lady Mouseykins, whom she had borne after the death of her seven elder sons, should have been slain by his hand, and when a lady had fallen in love with him deformed as he was. You must have actually seen young Drosselmeier about Christmas-time in his father's shop at Nuremberg—a Nutcracker truly, but also a prince in disguise. There, children, is the story of the hard nut, and now you know why people so often say "That was a hard nut to crack!" and how it comes that nutcrackers are so ugly.'

So ended the Counsellor's tale. Mary thought that Princess Pirlipat was a real nasty, thankless thing, but Fred assured her that if Nutcracker were a brave fellow, he would easily do for the Mouse King, and soon regain his former lovely figure.

CHAPTER X

Uncle and Nephew

If it ever happened to any of my honored hearers or readers to get cut by glass, he will know for himself how much it hurts, and what a bad thing it is altogether, since it takes so long to heal. Mary had to spend nearly a whole week in bed, and when she got up she felt quite light-headed. But in the end she grew well again, and could run about the room as merrily as ever.

The glass cupboard made a fine show, for there stood, all new and clean, the trees and flowers and toy-houses, and the beautiful, splendid dolls. First of all, Mary looked for her dear Nutcracker, who, from his place on the second shelf, smiled back to her with his teeth quite in good order. As she again so affectionately surveyed her favorite, it suddenly came into her troubled heart that all Godfather Drosselmeier's tale was nothing but the history of this Nutcracker and his feud with Lady Mouseykins and her son. Now she saw that her Nutcracker could be no other than young Drosselmeier of Nuremberg, the godfather's handsome nephew, so unhappily transformed by Lady Mouseykins. For, that the skillful Clockmaker of the Court of Pirlipat's father was nobody but Counsellor

Drosselmeier himself, Mary had never doubted for a moment, even while listening to the tale.

'But why did your uncle not help you? Why did he not help you?' lamented Mary, as she always more and more vividly conceived the idea that in that battle of which she had been a witness, Nutcracker's kingdom and crown were at stake. 'Were not all the other toys his subjects, and was it not sure that the Court Astronomer's prophecy would be fulfilled, and young Drosselmeier become King of Doll-land?'

Wise Mary went on turning the matter over in her mind till she believed that Nutcracker and his vassals had actually the life and motion which she attributed to them in her imagination. But it was not so. Everything in the cupboard remained stiffer and stiller than ever and Mary, resolutely clinging to her inner conviction, put the blame of this on the continued enchantment worked by Lady Mouseykins and her seven-headed son.

'Yet,' she said out loud to the Nutcracker, 'if you are not in a condition to move yourself, or to speak to me the least little word, I know, dear Mr. Drosselmeier, that you can understand me and my goodwill to you. So you may count on my assistance in the hour of need. At all events, I will ask your uncle to give you the aid of his skill where it is necessary.'

Nutcracker remained quiet and still but to Mary it seemed that a light sigh breathed through the cupboard door, the glass panes whispering almost inaudibly but in wondrously sweet tones, as if a small bell-note were singing:

'Mary mine,
Protectress dear,
I will be thine,
Oh, Mary dear!'

In the ice-cold shudder which came over her, Mary yet felt a strange joy.

Twilight now drew on. Her father entered the room with Godfather Drosselmeier. Then it was not long before Louisa set the dinner table and the family sat round it, talking pleasantly about all sorts of things.

Mary had quietly brought her small arm-chair and placed herself at the godfather's feet. When the others for a moment were silent, she looked with her great blue eyes right into the Counsellor's face, and said:

'I know now, dear godfather, that my Nutcracker is your nephew, the young Drosselmeier from Nuremberg. He has become a prince, or rather a king, so much has come true, as your companion, the Astronomer, prophesied. But you know well that he is at open war with Lady Mouseykin's son, the ugly Mouse King. Why don't you give him help?'

Mary further related the whole course of the battle as she had witnessed it, and was often interrupted by her mother and Louisa laughing at her. However, Fred and the Counsellor listened intently.

'Wherever did the girl get all that silly stuff into her head?' said the Doctor.

'Oh, she has a lively imagination,' answered her mother. 'These are just dreams which came from the feverishness after she hurt her arm.'

'It is all a lie, said Fred; 'my hussars are not such cowards!'

But Godfather Drosselmeier, smiling knowingly, took Mary on his lap, and spoke more softly than ever.

'Ah, my dear Mary, to you belongs a gift denied to me and to us all. You are a born princess like Pirlipat, for you reign in a beautiful bright kingdom! But you have much to suffer if you make the cause of poor deformed Nutcracker your own, for the Mouse King persecutes him in all ways. Yet you—not I—you alone can save him, if you will only be loyal and steadfast.'

Neither Mary nor any one else knew what Drosselmeier meant by these words. Indeed, they seemed to the Doctor so odd that he felt the Counsellor's pulse and said:

'My good friend, you must not feel well.'

But the Doctor's wife shook her head thoughtfully, and said half to herself:

'I can guess what the Counsellor means, though I can't put it into plain words.'

CHAPTER XI

The Victory

ot long afterwards, Mary was awakened one moonlit night by a strange commotion that seemed to come from one corner of the room. It was as if pebbles were being thrown and rolled about, amid a hideous accompaniment of hissing and squeaking.

'Ah, the mice! The mice are coming back!' cried Mary in terror, and would have waked her mother, but she could not utter a sound, or even move a finger, as she saw the Mouse King working himself through a hole in the wall, till at length, with sparkling eyes and shining crowns, he advanced into the room. Then, with a mighty bound he sprang up on the small table which stood close to Mary's bed.

'Hee! hee! hee! You must give me your sugar-plums, your toffee, small thing—or I will bite that Nutcracker of yours to pieces! Nutcracker, do you hear?'

So piped out the Mouse King, gnashing and clashing horribly with his teeth, and quickly sprang out of sight again through the mouse-hole.

Mary was so distressed by the dreadful apparition that next morning she looked quite pale, and could scarcely speak, being choked with fear. A hundred times she thought of telling what had happened, to her mother, or to Louisa, or at least to Fred but she asked herself, 'Will any of them believe me? I'm sure that I will be laughed at by everybody?'

Yet it was quite clear to her she must sacrifice her sugar-plums and toffee to save Nutcracker. As much as she had of these nice things she laid out that evening on the edge of the cupboard shelf. Next morning, her mother said:

'I don't know how the mice got into our parlor—just see, poor Mary, they have eaten up all your candy!'

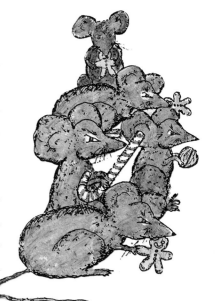

Indeed it was so! The sticky toffee had not proved much to the taste of greedy Mouse King, but he had nibbled all over it with his sharp teeth just for spite so that Mary wouldn't be able to eat any of it.

Mary did not take the loss of her sweets much to heart. Rather, she secretly rejoiced to think that it had saved Nutcracker's life. But what were her feelings when next night there came again a squeaking and squawking at her ear.

Ah! It was the Mouse King back again, and still more horribly glowed his eyes than the night before, and still more hatefully hissed he between his teeth:

'Must give me your sugar and gingerbread figures, little thing, or I bite your Nutcracker into pieces!' With this, away scampered the grim Mouse King.

In great distress, Mary went next morning to the cupboard, and sorrowfully looked at her sugar and gingerbread men. She had reason indeed to be sorrowful, for you can't think, my good reader, what beautiful little figures made out of sugar and gingerbread Mary Stahlbaum possessed. First of all, a very pretty shepherd with a shepherdess was feeding a whole herd of milkwhite sheep, and his dog jumped close by quite like life. Then came two postmen with letters in their hands, and four fine couples of nicely-dressed young men with maidens elegantly adorned all over, were rocking themselves in a swing. Behind some ballet-dancers stood Old King Cole beside the Maid of Orleans, for whom Mary did not care so very much.

Right back in the corner was a red-cheeked little child, her favorite of all, and realizing what was the candy child's hideous fate the tears sprang into Mary's eyes.

'Ah, dear Herr Drosselmeier!' she cried, turning to the Nutcracker, 'whatever will I not do to save you?'

Nutcracker the while looked so sad that Mary, who could fancy she saw the Mouse King's seven jaws open to devour the unhappy youth, resolved to sacrifice everything for his sake.

All her sugar figures she set out this evening on the edge of the shelf, as before she had done with the candy. She kissed the shepherd, the shepherdess, the little lambs, and last of all she fetched from the corner her favorite, the dear red-cheeked child, whom she took care to put behind all the rest. The gingerbread Old King Cole and the Maid of Orleans had to stand in the first row.

'Oh, this is too bad!' exclaimed her mother, next morning. 'There must be a great nasty mouse living in the cupboard, for all poor Mary's pretty sugar figures are gnawed and bitten to bits.'

Mary could hardly keep back her tears, but she soon smiled again at the thought, 'What does it matter so long as Nutcracker is safe!'

In the evening, when her mother told the Counsellor about the mischief a mouse did in the children's cupboard, Dr. Stahlbaum remarked what a pity it was they could not get rid of this pest, which played such tricks in the cupboard and ate up Mary's sweet things.

'Well,' put in Fred eagerly, 'the baker, who lives below us, has a fine gray "chamber councillor," which I can bring up. He will soon stop these doings, and bite off the mouse's head, were it Lady Mouseykins herself, or her son, the Mouse King!'

'Yes, by jumping about on chairs and tables,' laughed his mother, 'and upsetting cups and glasses, and doing ever so much more damage.'

'Not at all!' answered Fred. 'The baker's cat is a clever fellow. I wish I could walk as steadily along the sharp roof as he can.'

'Only let us have no cats at night,' begged Louisa, who could not bear cats.

'Fred is right,' said his father. 'But first we might try setting a trap, have we none?'

'We can get the best kind from Godfather Drossel-meier, who invented them!' cried Fred, causing general laughter.

The mistress declared that there was no trap in the house. The Counsellor said he had several, and sent at once for a first-class one.

Their godfather's story of the Hard Nut came now clearly into the mind of Mary and Fred. While Betsy, the cook, was toasting the bacon, Mary trembled with excitement, and, her head full of the story and its marvels, spoke excitedly:

'Ah, Lady Queen, do beware of Mouseykins and her family!'

But Fred had drawn his sword, bidding the whole race of mice come on, and he would soon clear them off.

All, however, remained still, under and about the hearthstone. When now the Counsellor tied the shred of bacon on a thin thread, and ever so softly laid the trap in the cupboard, Fred called out, 'Take care, God-father Clockmaker, that the Mouse King doesn't play a trick on you.'

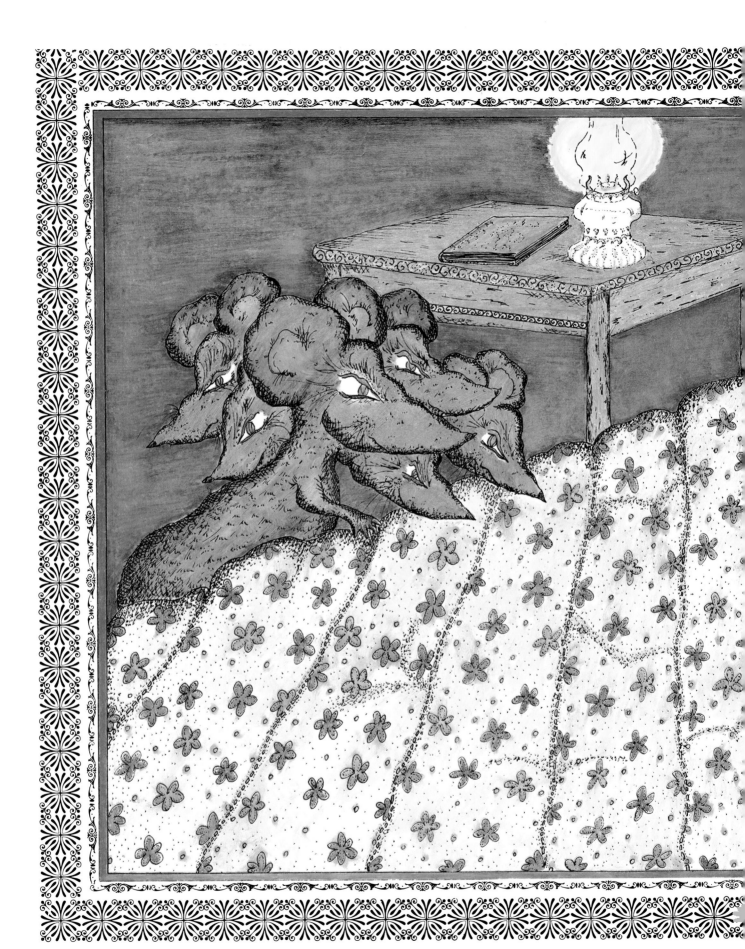

Ah, what had poor Mary to go through that night! There came an ice-cold creeping up and down her arm, and a loathsome breath on her cheek, and a piping and squeaking in her ear. The horrible Mouse King sat on her shoulder, blood-red foam dripping out of his seven open jaws, and, with gnashing and clashing teeth, he hissed out to Mary as she lay motionless for fear and dread:

> 'Hiss! Hiss! none of your bacon!
> Mouse King too sharp, not to be taken!
> Trap very fine, but not what it looks!
> Give me out now your picture-books!
> Do you hear?—and your new frock too!
> Else there shall be no peace for you!
> You very well know,
> Nutcracker must go,
> I will tear him so—
> Hee! Hee!—Pi! Pi! Squeak! Squeak!'

Now was Mary overcome by sorrow and woe. She looked so pale and bewildered that when her mother next morning remarked that the mouse had not been caught, believing Mary to be afraid of it and distressed about the loss of her sweets, she added:

'But never mind, dear child, we will soon get rid of the naughty mouse. If traps are no good, Fred must bring up the baker's cat.'

As soon as Mary found herself alone in the parlor, she went up to the glass cupboard, and, sobbing, spoke thus to her Nutcracker:

'Ah, my dear, good Mr. Drosselmeier, what can a poor unhappy girl do for you? Were I to give all my picture-books, even my beautiful new dress which I got as a Christmas present, to be torn to pieces by the horrible Mouse King, he would still go on asking for more and more, so that at last I shall have nothing left to give, and he will want to devour me instead of you. Please help me, I have run out of plans. What am I to do now?'

Despite weeping and lamenting so bitterly, Mary noticed that through the night a great spot of blood had been left on Nutcracker's neck. Ever since she became convinced that her Nutcracker was, in truth, young Drosselmeier, the Counsellor's nephew, she had given up carrying him in her arms. She no longer cuddled and kissed him. Indeed, out of a certain shyness she hardly liked to touch him. Yet now she took him very carefully out of the cupboard, and began to rub the blood spot from his neck with her pocket-handkerchief.

But to her amazement, she all at once felt Nutcracker growing warm in her hands and begin to move his limbs. Quickly she set him back in the cupboard, where his little mouth waggled shakingly up and down, and painfully he lisped out:

'Ah, most worthy Miss Stahlbaum, devoted friend, how can I thank you for all you have done! You are right! No picture book, or Christmas frock will satisfy the fiendish Mouse King. Procure me only a sword—a sword, and I will answer for the rest, let him do his worst!'

Here Nutcracker's speech died away, and his eyes, lately animated by an expression of inward grief, became again fixed and dull as glass.

Mary felt no horror. Rather, she skipped for joy, now knowing the means to save Nutcracker without further sore sacrifices. But wherever was she to get a sword for the small man?

She resolved to take Fred into council, and that evening, their parents having gone out, as these two sat together in the parlor by the glass cupboard, she told him all that had happened to her with Nutcracker and Mouse King, and what was now required for the former's deliverance.

Nothing of all this made such impression on Fred as how, according to Mary's report, his hussars had behaved themselves so badly in the battle. He just asked very seriously, whether things had really gone as she said and when she assured him on her word that it was so, he went at once to the cupboard and addressed his hussars with a moving speech. Then, as a punishment for their selfishness and cowardice he cut the emblems

off their hats, one after another, and forbade them to play the Hussar-Guards' March for a year. His reprimand ended, he turned to Mary, saying:

'As for the sword, I can supply Nutcracker, for yesterday I pensioned off an old colonel of cuirassiers, who does not need his sword any more.'

The said colonel was enjoying the pension assigned him by Fred in a back corner of the top shelf. Thence being fetched down, his smart silver-mounted sword was taken off him and hung round the waist of Nutcracker.

That night Mary could not sleep for anxious dread. At midnight she thought she could hear in the parlor a strange stir, a clang, a confusion. All of a sudden it went *squeak!*

'The Mouse King, the Mouse King!' cried Mary, and sprang, startled, out of bed.

All was still, but soon there came a soft, soft tapping at the door, and a tiny voice made itself heard.

'Dearest Miss Stahlbaum, now you can be at ease—good, joyful news!'

Mary, recognizing the voice of young Drosselmeier, threw on her dress and hurriedly opened the door. Outside of it stood little Nutcracker, the dripping sword in his right hand, a candle in his left. As soon as he saw Mary, he knelt down on one knee, and spoke thus:

'You alone, my lady, are she who filled my heart with courage, and gave my arm strength to combat the haughty foe that dared insult you! Conquered lies the traitorous Mouse King, and wallows in his blood. Scorn not, O lady, to receive the tokens of victory at the hands of your till-death-devoted knight!'

With this, Nutcracker pulled off the seven golden crowns of the Mouse King, strung round his left arm, and handed them over to Mary, who received them with delight. Then, rising to his feet, he went on:

'Ah, my dearest Miss Stahlbaum, having now overpowered my enemy, what wonderful things will I show you, if you would only have the kindness to follow me a little way. Please do, oh please do, dear young lady!'

CHAPTER XII

The Toy-Kingdom

None of you children, I believe, would have hesitated about following the noble, good-hearted Nutcracker, who had only the best of intentions. Mary consented the more willingly, as she knew well what a great claim she had upon Nutcracker's gratitude, and felt sure he would keep his word, and would show her some splendid things. So she answered:

'I will go with you, Mr. Drosselmeier, but it must not be far or for long, as I have not slept nearly enough.'

'On that account,' replied Nutcracker, 'I take the nearest way, though a somewhat difficult one.'

Forward he strode, and Mary after him, till he stopped before a huge old clothes closet standing on the floor. To her astonishment, Mary observed that the door of this usually locked closet was open and she quite plainly saw her father's fur coat hanging right in front. Nutcracker cleverly climbed up the braidings and trimmings of it, till he could catch hold of a large tassel dangling by a thick cord on the back of the fur. As soon as he had given this tassel a strong pull, through the sleeves of the cloak came down an elegant cedar-wood staircase.

'Will you please accompany me up the stair my dearest young lady?' said Nutcracker.

Mary did so, then scarcely had she mounted through the sleeves to the collar, when a dazzling light streamed into her eyes, and all at once she found herself on a delightfully-scented meadow, from which rose millions of sparks like gleaming gems.

'We are now on Sugar-candy meadow,' said Nutcracker, 'but will at once pass through that gate.'

Now, as Mary looked, she was aware of a beautiful gate, which rose on the meadow only a few steps before them. It seemed to be all built of white marble, dotted with brown and raisin-colored patches, but, on coming nearer, Mary saw clearly that the whole mass consisted of almonds and raisins baked together in sugar, for which reason, Nutcracker informed her, the gate they were about to pass through was named the Almond and Raisin Gate.

In a covered passage leading out from this gate, apparently built of barley-sugar, six little monkeys dressed in red jackets were making the most beautiful music from cymbals and triangles that was ever heard, so that Mary scarcely noticed how she advanced on the marble flags, which were nothing else than an elegantly polished mosaic of sugar-plums. Soon rose about them a very sweet smell, given forth by a wonderful wood that opened out on both sides. In the shady glade was such a bright sparkling and glittering that it could be plainly seen how gold and silver fruit hung on the brightly-colored stems, and how trunks and branches were all adorned with ribbons and nosegays, like the guests at a joyful wedding party. And when the scent of oranges stirred as a rising breeze, there was a whispering through leaves and twigs, and the tinsel rustled and rattled, so that it all sounded like merry music, to the tune of which the shining little flames kept hopping and dancing.

'Ah, how lovely it is here!' cried Mary, enraptured with pleasure.

'We are in Christmas-tree Wood, dear miss,' said Nutcracker.

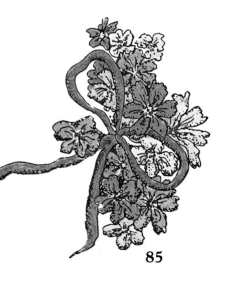

85

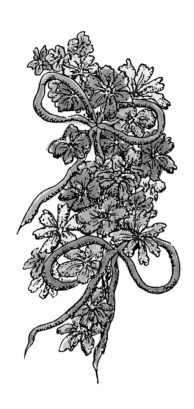

'Oh!' went on Mary, 'if I only might stay here a little! It is so beautiful!'

Nutcracker clapped his little hands, and with that came forward some small shepherds and shepherdesses, hunters and huntresses, who looked so frail and white that one could believe them made of pure sugar, but Mary, though they were wandering through the wood, had not yet noticed them. They brought out an ornate little arm-chair, all made of gold, laid a cushion of liquorice upon it, and very politely invited Mary to sit down. As soon as she had done so, the shepherds and shepherdesses performed a very graceful dance, for which the hunters blew a tune in quite correct style, and then they all disappeared into the underbush.

'You will excuse them, most worthy Miss Stahlbaum,' said Nutcracker, 'you will excuse their dance going off so badly. These people all work upon strings, and must always keep on doing the same thing, and if the hunters played so sleepily and flat, there are reasons also for that. The sugar-basket was indeed hanging over their heads in the Christmas-tree, but rather out of their reach. Shall we not now go on a little farther?'

'Ah, but it was all very pretty, and pleased me very much,' said Mary, as she got up and followed Nutcracker going on in front.

Their course lay along a sweet rippling, murmuring brook, out of which seemed to rise rich odors that filled the whole wood.

'It is the Orange-brook,' said Nutcracker, in answer to her inquiry, 'yet, apart from its fine scent, it is nothing for size and beauty to the Lemonade Stream, that likewise falls into the Coconut-milk Sea.'

In fact, Mary soon caught a stronger sound of rushing and dashing, and came in sight of the broad Lemonade Stream, whose noble gray-tinted waves wound their way through a glowing greenwood lighted up with glowing garnet stones. A singularly fresh, bracing coolness was exhaled by this splendid water. Not far off there rolled slowly past them a dull yellow stream, that sent out an uncommonly sweet smell, on the banks of which sat all

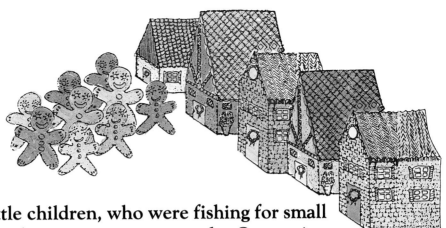

sorts of pretty little children, who were fishing for small thick fish, and ate them up as soon as caught. On coming nearer, Mary remarked that these fish looked like filberts. Some little way up this stream lay a very nice village: houses, barns, church, parsonage, all dark brown, with smart gilded roofs, and many of the walls were colored, as if citron-peel and almond kernels had been stuck in them.

'That,' said Nutcracker, 'is Gingerbreadham, which lies on Honeyburn. Some very pretty people live there, but they are mostly in low spirits, because they suffer much from toothache, so we will keep away from it.'

Just then Mary perceived another little town, which consisted of nothing but gaily-tinted, transparent houses, and was most beautiful to look at.

Nutcracker went straight towards it and now Mary heard a wild cheery din, and saw how a thousand dwarf-ish folk were in the act of examining and unloading many high-packed waggons which stood in the market-place. But what they took out of these waggons appeared nothing but bright-colored papers, and the silver coverings of chocolate sticks.

'We are in Bonbonstown,' said Nutcracker, 'and there has just arrived a convoy sent from Paperland by the Chocolate King. The poor people of Bonbonstown have recently been seriously threatened by the Fly-Sultan's army, on which account they are covering their houses with the supplies from Paperland, and throwing up forti-fications of the strong materials which the Chocolate King sends them. But, dear Miss Stahlbaum, we will not visit all the small towns and villages of this country—on to the capital!—to the capital!'

CHAPTER XIII

The Capital of Toyland

utcracker rushed forward, and Mary after him, full of curiosity. Before long, a rich perfume of roses greeted them, and all the air seemed filled with soft waving rose tints. Mary saw that this was the reflection of a rose-red shining river, whose rosily silver ripples murmured and prattled before her as if keeping time and melody. On this lovely water, that gradually spread out into a lake, swam noble silver-white swans with golden bands round their necks that sang the most beautiful songs, each trying to outdo the other, to the tune of which little diamond fishes ducked up and down through the rose-water as in a merry dance.

'Ah,' cried Mary, quite excited, 'this is really the lake which Godfather Drosselmeier once promised to make for me, and I myself am the girl who is to play with the darling swans!'

Nutcracker gave such a scornful laugh as she had never heard him do, and said:

'A thing like this can your godfather never manufacture! Don't you trouble about that, however, but let us sail over the Rose Lake to the capital city on the other side.'

The little Nutcracker again clapped his small hands, and then the Rose Lake grew more agitated. The waves washed higher on the shore, and Mary saw coming towards her from the distance a boat or floating chariot, in the form of a shell, like one glowing, sun-bright, sparkling gem, drawn along by two gold-scaled dolphins. Twelve dear little island people dressed in caps and apron like gowns woven out of humming-birds' feathers, sprang on shore, and carried first Mary, then Nutcracker, softly passing over the waves, into the boat.

Oh, how nice it was when Mary drove off through the rose spray and the rose waves! The two gold-scaled dolphins lifted up their heads and spouted crystal jets high into the air and, as they fell back in gleaming and sparkling rainbows, two sweet voices, like little bells of silver, seemed to be singing:

'Who sails upon the rosy sea?
A darling fairy it must be!
Swans, ta, ta!
Goldfinch, tra la!
Stream, run low!
Winds soft blow!
All peace to-day!
For here comes a fairy.'

But the twelve little islanders, who had jumped up on the back of the chariot, appeared not to like the singing of the water jets, for they kept shaking their parasols, so that the date-palm leaves, of which these were made, rattled and rustled, and at the same time the whole twelve stamped with their feet to an odd kind of tune, and sang for their part:

'Clack, click! click, clack!
Up and down! down and up!
Island boys like a noise!
Fish jump! Swans flap!
Shell-boat rumble! jumble! tumble!
Up and down! down and up!
Click, clack! clack, click!'

'These fellows are very funny people,' said Nut-

cracker, somewhat put out by their din, 'but they will set the whole lake in an uproar if they go on so.'

Indeed, there soon broke loose a confused tumult of extraordinary voices, which seemed to be floating all around in the air and the water. Yet Mary did not mind them, but looked hard down into the scented rose waves, out of which a sweet, pleasant girl's face smiled back at her.

'Ah,' she cried joyfully, clapping her little hands. 'Ah, just look, Mr. Drosselmeier! Down there is the Princess Pirlipat, who smiles at me so graciously!—Do look, dear Mr. Drosselmeier!'

But Nutcracker sighed almost mournfully, and said:

'Oh, dearest Miss Stahlbaum, that is not the Princess Pirlipat, that is always and only yourself, always only your own pretty face, that smiles so sweetly out of the rose waves.'

At this Mary quickly drew her head back, shut her eyes tight, and felt much ashamed. Next moment she was lifted out of the shell-boat and carried on shore by the twelve island children. She found herself in a small thicket, almost more beautiful than the Christmas-tree wood, so brightly did everything here shine and glitter. Especially admirable were the foreign fruits that hung on all the trees, and were not only of striking colors but also had a wonderfully fine aroma.

'This is Confection Grove,' Nutcracker told her; 'but there is the capital!'

What now did Mary see? How shall I attempt to describe to you, dear children, the beauty and splendor of the city, which stretched itself far over a flowery plain before her eyes? Not only were the walls and towers gay with the most striking colors, but the form of the buildings was such as you never saw on earth. For, instead of thatch, the houses had beautifully-carved crowns on the top of them, and the towers were capped by the most lovely gay garlands ever seen, like the ornaments of a wedding cake.

When they passed through the gate, which looked as if it were built of macaroons and candied fruit, a band of silver-papered soldiers presented arms, and a little man in a brocaded dressing-gown threw his arms round Nutcracker's neck with the words:

'Welcome, noble Prince, welcome to Confectionerbury!'

Mary was not a little astonished to see young Drosselmeier recognized as a prince by this highly-distinguished person. But now she heard a confused outburst of tiny voices mingling, together, such a cheering and laughing, such a playing and singing, that she could think of nothing else, and asked the little Nutcracker what this meant.

'Oh, my good Miss Stahlbaum,' answered he, 'this is nothing remarkable! Confectionerbury is a prosperous, lively city, and every day some kind of amusement goes on here. But be pleased to come a little farther.'

A few steps brought them out upon the great marketplace, which presented a splendid sight. All the houses round it were of open sugar work, story rising over story. In the middle stood a tall sugar-coated cake, like a monument, and on each side of this a very skillfully made fountain spouted in the air lemonade, gingerbeer, and other nice drinks, while into the basins below ran pure rich cream which you might spoon up at once without any further trouble. But prettier than all were the dear little people who swarmed round by the thousands in and out, cheering and laughing, and joking and singing, in short, raising that merry din which Mary had already heard from some way off. There were finely-dressed ladies and gentlemen, Arabs and Greeks, Highlanders and Indians, officers and soldiers, shepherds and sailors, grand Turks and tomfools, harlequins and columbines, in fact all kinds of people you find in the world.

At one corner the tumult grew greater. The people thronged together, for just then the Grand Mogul had himself carried by in a litter attended by three-and-ninety grandees of his realm, and by seven hundred slaves. But it happened that at the other corner the Guild of Fishermen, five hundred strong, were holding their

festival. It was a pity that at the very same time, the Turkish Sultan had the idea of taking a ride over the market-place with three thousand of his elite troops, and yet another solemn procession, clanging and chorusing, crowded round the cake tree. What a pressing and pushing and shoving and quarreling then came about! Soon, too, there were many cries of distress, for in the crush a fisherman had knocked off a Brahmin's head, and the Grand Mogul was nearly upset by a tomfool.

Wilder and wilder rose the din and the crowds were already falling to blows. Suddenly, the man in a brocaded gown who at the gate had greeted Nutcracker as prince, climbed up on the cake tree, and, after three times ringing a very clear tinkling bell, call out thrice:

'Confectioner! Confectioner! Confectioner!'

At once the tumult was calmed, every one trying to escape from the confusion as best he could. Finally, when the entangled processions had gotten clear of each other, the muddied Grand Mogul had been brushed clean, and the Brahmin's head set on again, the merry uproar broke forth anew.

'What does it mean, that *Confectioner*, dear Mr. Drosselmeier?' asked Mary.

'Ah, my good Miss Stahlbaum,' answered Nutcracker, 'Confectioner is the name given here to an unknown but very dreadful power, of which people believe that it can do with them what it will! It is the Fate that rules over this little merry folk, and they fear it so much, that through the mere mention of its name, the greatest tumult can be appeased, as Mr. Burgermaster has just shown us. Every one then thinks no more of earthly things, of pushes in the ribs, and bumps on the head, but retires into himself and asks seriously, "What is man, and what will become of him?" '

Mary could not restrain a loud cry of wonder, nay, of the highest amazement, when she all at once saw standing before her, bathed in rosy light, a brightly-lighted castle with a hundred magnificent towers. Here and there the walls were decorated with rich bouquets of violets, lilies, tulips, stocks, and the like, the duller tints of which set off the dazzling white of the ground-work shimmering in rosy light. The great dome of the central building, as well as the pyramid-formed caps of the towers, were dotted with thousands of sparkling gold and silver stars.

'Now we are before Marzipan Castle,' said Nutcracker.

Mary was quite overwhelmed by the view of this enchanted palace, yet she did not fail to notice that the summit of one great tower was wholly missing. There was a gang of small puppets standing on a scaffold of cinnamon sticks, seemingly engaged in restoring the missing tower. Even before she could ask Nutcracker the meaning of this, he went on:

'A short time ago this fine castle was exposed to serious danger, if not utter destruction. The Giant Guzzle, happening to pass by, bit one tower right off, and was already gnawing at the great dome when the Confectionerbury people brought him a whole quarter of their city as tribute, and a good slice of Jamshire as well. With this he consented to be fed off, and went his ways.'

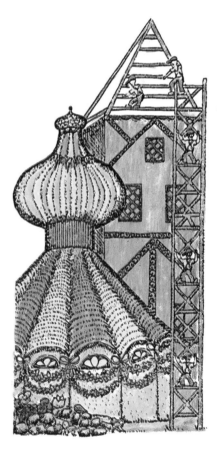

At this moment a soft pleasing strain of music was heard, the gate of the castle opened, and out stepped twelve small pages bearing lighted cloves in their hands by way of torches. Their heads consisted of a single pearl, their bodies of rubies and emeralds, and so they walked along very fine upon little feet of pure gold. They were followed by four ladies, almost as large as Mary's doll Clara, but so extraordinarily majestic and gorgeously arrayed, that not for a single moment could Mary mistake them for anything but born Princesses.

'Oh, my Prince!—oh, my dear Prince!—oh, my brother!' they exclaimed, embracing Nutcracker in the tenderest manner, and one could not be sure whether they were about to laugh or to cry for joy.

Nutcracker seemed to be much moved. He wiped away a stream of tears from his eyes, took Mary by the hand, and spoke movingly:

'This is Miss Mary Stahlbaum, the daughter of a most respectable physician, and the preserver of my life. Had she not thrown her slipper at the right time, had she not furnished me with the sword of the pensioned cuirassier colonel, I should now be lying in my grave, bitten to pieces by the accursed Mouse King. Oh, this Miss Stahlbaum! Tell me, is Pirlipat, even though a Princess by birth, her equal in beauty, heart, and virtue? No! I say—no!'

'No!' cried all the ladies, embracing Mary and sobbing out, 'Oh, you noble preserver of our dear princely brother—excellent Miss Stahlbaum!'

Now the ladies led Mary and Nutcracker within the castle, and into a hall, the walls of which were of clear sparkling and glowing crystal. But what pleased Mary above all the rest was the dearest little chairs, tables, sofas, and so forth, standing round about, which were made of cedar or mahogany wood, inlaid with gold flowers. The Princesses requested Mary and Nutcracker to sit down, and said that they themselves would at once get a meal ready. Then they brought out a number of little pots and dishes made of the finest Japanese porcelain, also spoons, knives, and forks, graters, stew-pans, and other kitchen utensils of gold and silver. Next they brought out the most beautiful fruits and spices such as Mary had never seen. Then, in the most elegant manner, with their small snow-white hands, they began to peel the fruit, pound the spices, rub down the sugar-sticks, in short, play the housewife, that Mary could well see how these Princesses were at home in the kitchen, and what a rich meal was to be set before her.

Feeling conscious that she could show herself mistress of such matters, she secretly wished the Princesses would give her a hand in their work. As if she had guessed Mary's wish, the most beautiful of Nutcracker's sisters passed over to her a small gold mortar, with the words:

'Oh, sweet friend, dear preserver of my brother, please break a little bit off this sugar-stick!'

While Mary now pounded away in the mortar so heartily that it sounded quite pleasant, as if a pretty tune were being chimed forth, Nutcracker began to relate in

full how the grim battle between his army and the Mouse King's had gone. He explained how he had been beaten through the cowardice of his troops, and how the hateful Mouse King would have bitten him all to pieces, but for the fact that Mary had sacrificed many of her subjects, persons in her service and the like to preserve his safety. During this narrative it seemed to Mary as if his words, even her own strokes in the mortar, grew fainter and stranger. Soon she saw the silver floor rising up like thin clouds of mist, in which floated the Princesses, the pages, Nutcracker and her own self. Her ears were filled with a queer singing, ringing and burning that died away in the distance. Now she rose upon swelling waves higher and higher—higher and higher—higher and higher—!

CHAPTER XIV

Conclusion

P R-R—puff! Down fell Mary from a measureless height. That was a fall! But at once she opened her eyes, and there she lay on her little bed, in clear daylight, and her mother stood beside her, saying:

'How can you sleep so long? Breakfast has been ready long ago!'

You take notice, honored reader, that Mary, quite bewildered by all the wonderful things she saw, had at last fallen asleep in the hall of Marzipan Castle. Clearly the boys, or the pages, or the Princesses, with their own hands, must have brought her home and put her to bed.

'Oh, mother, dear mother, young Mr. Drosselmeier has taken me through the night to see many fine and amazing sights!'

Then she told the whole story almost exactly as I have just told it, and her mother looked at her in amazement.

'Dear Mary,' said her mother, when she came to an end, 'you have had a long, beautiful dream, but now shake all that out of your head.'

Mary obstinately stuck to her belief that she had not been dreaming, but had really seen all this. So her mother took her to the glass cupboard, brought down Nutcracker from the third shelf where he stood as usual, and said:

'How can you, silly child, believe that these wooden figures from Nuremberg are alive and able to move of themselves?'

'But, dear mother,' broke in Mary, 'I know very well that the small Nutcracker is young Mr. Drosselmeier of Nuremberg, Godfather Drosselmeier's nephew.'

At this both her father and mother broke into a loud peal of laughter.

'Ah,' Mary went on, almost in tears, 'now you are laughing at my Nutcracker, dear father. Yet he spoke so well of you, for when we came to Marzipan Castle and he introduced me to the Princesses, his sisters, he said you were a very respectable physician!'

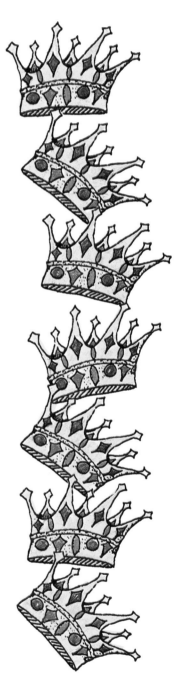

Louder still was the laughter, in which Louisa joined, and even Fred. Then Mary ran into the next room, made haste to bring out of her small treasure-box the seven crowns of the Mouse King, and handed them to her mother, with:

'Just see there—these are the Mouse King's seven crowns, which last night young Drosselmeier presented to me as tokens of his victory.'

With astonishment the doctor's wife examined the little crowns, which were so skillfully made out of a very bright metal quite unfamiliar to her, that they seemed the work of no human hands. The Doctor, too, took a good long look at them, and both father and mother seriously urged Mary to confess how she had come by these crowns. But she continued to stand by what she had said, and when her father grew stern with her, even scolded her as a little story-teller, she began to cry bitterly, and to lament:

'Ah, poor child that I am, what else can I say!'

At that moment the door opened. In walked the Counsellor, calling out:

'What's the matter? My godchild Mary crying and sobbing! What's the matter? What's the matter?'

The Doctor told him the whole story, showing him

the little crowns. No sooner had the Counsellor set eyes on them than he laughed, and said:

'Silly stuff! Silly stuff! These are the charms which long ago I used to wear on my watch-chain, and I gave them to Mary as a present on her birthday when she was two years old. Didn't you know them again?'

Neither the Doctor nor his wife remembered them. But, when Mary saw that the faces of her parents had become friendly again, she sprang upon Godfather Drosselmeier with the cry:

'Ah, Godfather, you know all about it. Do tell them yourself that my Nutcracker is your nephew, the young Herr Drosselmeier from Nuremberg, and that he gave me the little crowns!'

'Stupid, silly stuff!' muttered the Counsellor. Then her mother made Mary stand before her, and spoke very seriously:

'Just listen to me, Mary, you must put all these fancies and absurdities out of your head. If you say again that this common misshaped Nutcracker is the nephew of Mr. Counsellor, I will not only throw Nutcracker out of the window, but also all the rest of your toys, Missy Clara too.'

Now, indeed, poor Mary could no longer speak of that which filled her whole mind, for you may well suppose that such splendid and beautiful things as had happened to her are not to be forgotten. Even Fred turned his back on her when she tried to tell him of the wonderful land in which she had been so fortunate. He is said even to have whispered 'Silly goose!' at her. But the good nature he showed at other times will not let me believe this. Yet so much is certain, that, since he no longer put any faith in Mary's story, he formally, on open parade, retracted the wrong done to his hussars. As a token he gave them, instead of their lost emblems, much higher and finer feathers from a goose-quill, and permitted them to play the Hussar-Guards' March again. Well, we know what courage these hussars had shown when the mouse balls came whistling at their red waistcoats!

Mary might speak no more of her adventure, but that marvellous fairy kingdom still hovered round her in sweetly fleeting visions and beautiful echoes. She saw all of its glories once more as soon as she fixed her mind on the remembrance of them. And so it came about that, instead of playing as she used to do, she would sit still and silent, her thoughts far away, till everybody found fault with her for a little dreamer.

It happened that, as the Counsellor was one day mending a clock in her father's house, Mary sat before the glass cupboard, deep in her dreams, looking at Nutcracker, and she could not help bursting out aloud:

'Ah, dear Mr. Drosselmeier, if you were really alive, I would not behave like Princess Pirlipat and despise you, when you, for my sake, had ceased to be a handsome young man!'

'Eh! Eh! Silly stuff!' exclaimed the Counsellor. Then at that moment there came such a crack and a jerk, that Mary tumbled fainting from her chair.

When she came to herself again, her mother was petting her and saying:

'How could you tumble from your chair—such a big girl! Here is the nephew of the Counsellor come from Nuremberg, so you must be nice and well behaved.'

She looked up and saw that the Counsellor had again put on his glass wig and his drab coat, and was smiling very agreeably. In his hand he held a small but well-formed young man. He wore a fine red coat laced with gold, white silk stockings and pumps, and had stuck in his bosom a most beautiful nosegay. Most elegantly curled and powdered, and behind his back his hair hung done up in a pony-tail. The little sword by his side seemed to be all jewels, it glittered so, and the small hat under his arm was woven out of silk.

The young man lost no time in showing what pleasant manners he had, for he gave Mary a quantity of splendid playthings, especially the most lovely toffee and the same figures as the Mouse King had bitten to pieces. For Fred he had brought a wonderful fine sword. At table the polite visitor cracked nuts for the whole party. The

hardest could not withstand him. With his right hand he stuck them in his mouth, with his left he pulled up his head—crack!—the nut fell in pieces!

Mary blushed rose red as she looked at the nice young man, and she became still redder when, after dinner, young Drosselmeier invited her to go with him to the glass cupboard in the parlor.

'Play prettily together, then, children,' said the Counsellor, 'I have no objection, as all my clocks are now in order.'

But as soon as young Drosselmeier found himself alone with Mary, he knelt upon one knee and spoke thus:

'Ah, my dearest Miss Stahlbaum! You see here at your feet the fortunate man whose life you saved on this very spot. You were good enough to say that you would not despise me, as that ungrateful Princess Pirlipat did, if I became hideous for your sake. Now I am no more a common Nutcracker, but have received again my original, not unpleasing form. Oh, excellent young lady, bestow upon me your precious hand. Share with me my crown and kingdom. Reign with me in Marzipan Castle, for there now am I King!'

Mary raised the youth to his feet, and said softly:

'Dear Mr. Drosselmeier, you are a good-natured, kind-hearted man, and you also reign over a delightful land with very pretty, amusing people, so I take you for my husband!'

So then Mary and Drosselmeier became at once betrothed. When the engagement had lasted a year, he is said to have fetched her away in a gold coach drawn by silver horses. At the wedding danced two-and-twenty thousand of the most splendid of puppets decked out in pearls and diamonds, and Mary is now Queen of a country in which sparkling Christmas-tree woods, transparent Toffee Palaces, in short, the finest and most wonderful of things, are everywhere to be seen by those who have only eyes to see them.

So ends the story of Nutcracker and Mouse King.